SAGE ESCAPE
ADULT COLORING BOOK

Cover art and interior illustration by

Damian S Simankowicz

facebook.com/damianssimankowiczart
instagram.com/damianssimankowicz

SAGE ESCAPE: ADULT COLORING BOOK. First published in 2017 by Primal Archetype, this release 2021.

Published by Primal Archetype. Artwork © Damian S Simankowicz.

ISBN: 978-0-9942549-2-4

HOW TO USE THIS BOOK

Time to unwind and take a break from it all.
Grab your tools of choice (color pencils, crayons or markers),
put on your favorite tunes or just enjoy the silence,
and let your creativity take you away!

Choose from simple artwork to more complex pieces based on your mood. There are dozens of images ranging from aliens to robots, super soldiers, spaceships and much more!

This book has been created with single sided pages to help protect your artwork. You can also put a piece of card behind the image that you are coloring (especially if you are using markers).

Experiment, there's no one right way, so just have a good time. Feel free to cut out pages for displaying. Or even dismantle the book to share with friends.

And most importantly, have fun!

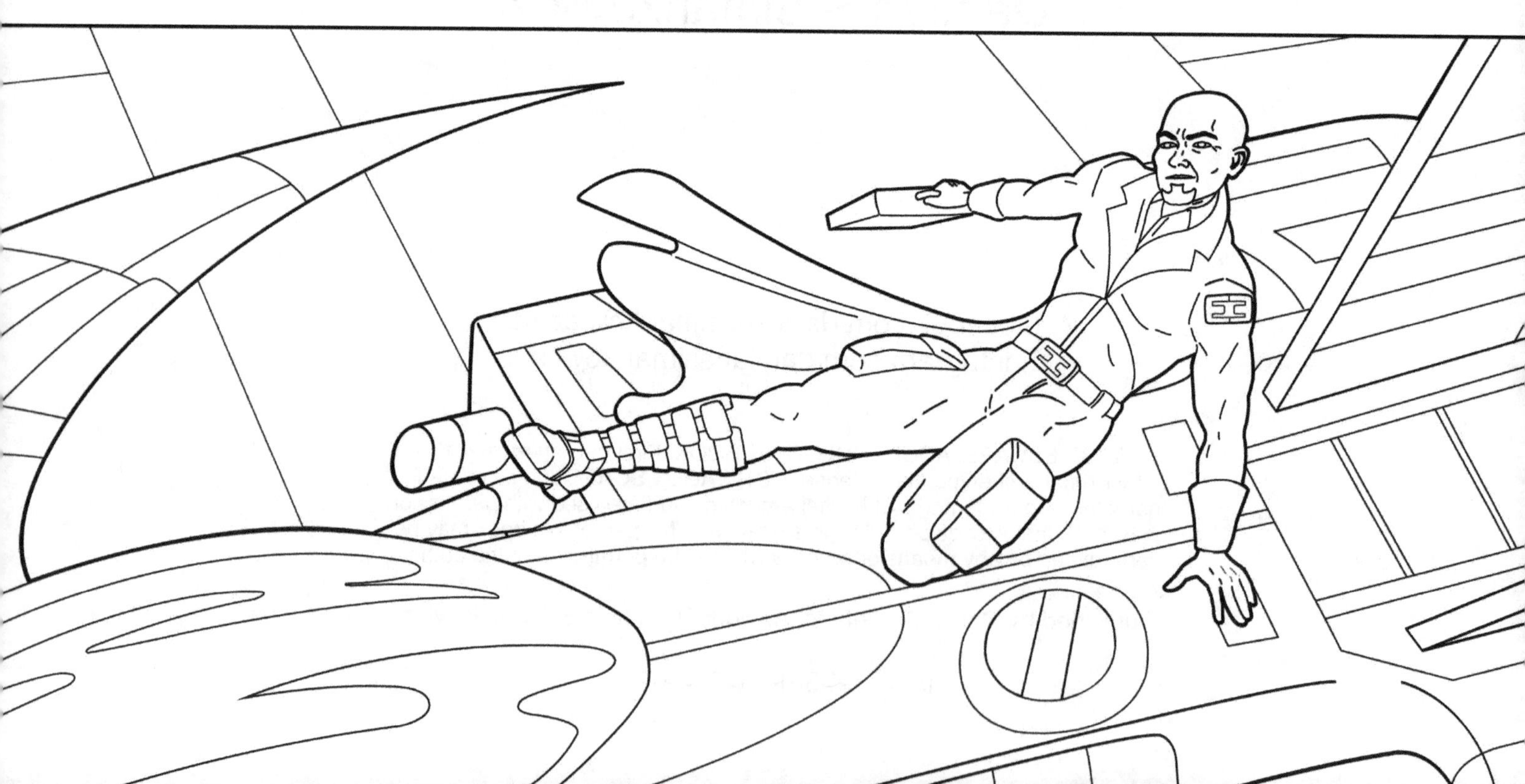

PRACTICE PAGE

Do you have some colors you'd like to try out? Or some techniques?
Or just need to warm up? Here's a page just for that!

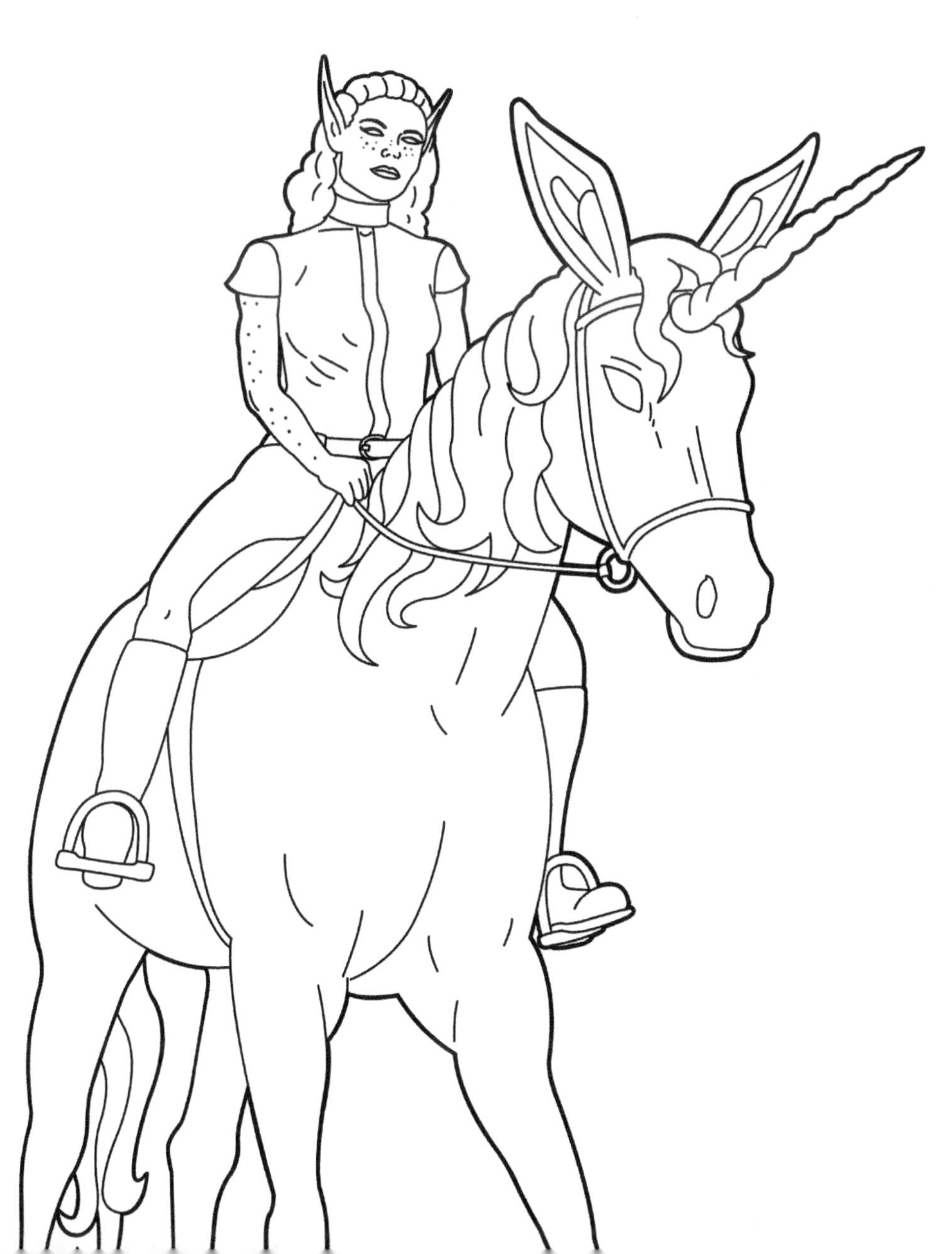

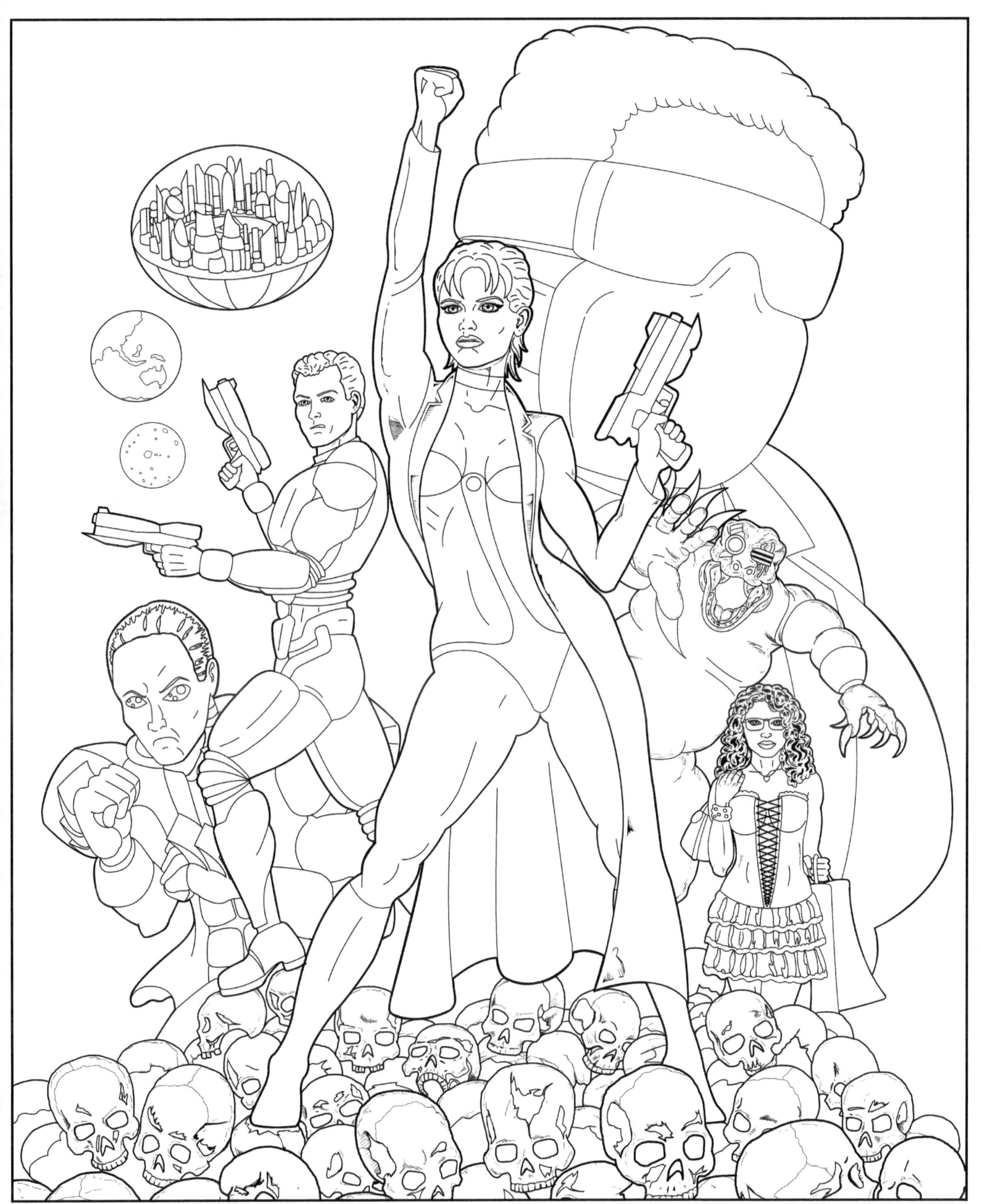

Sage is a human female that has been upgraded with military cybernetics.

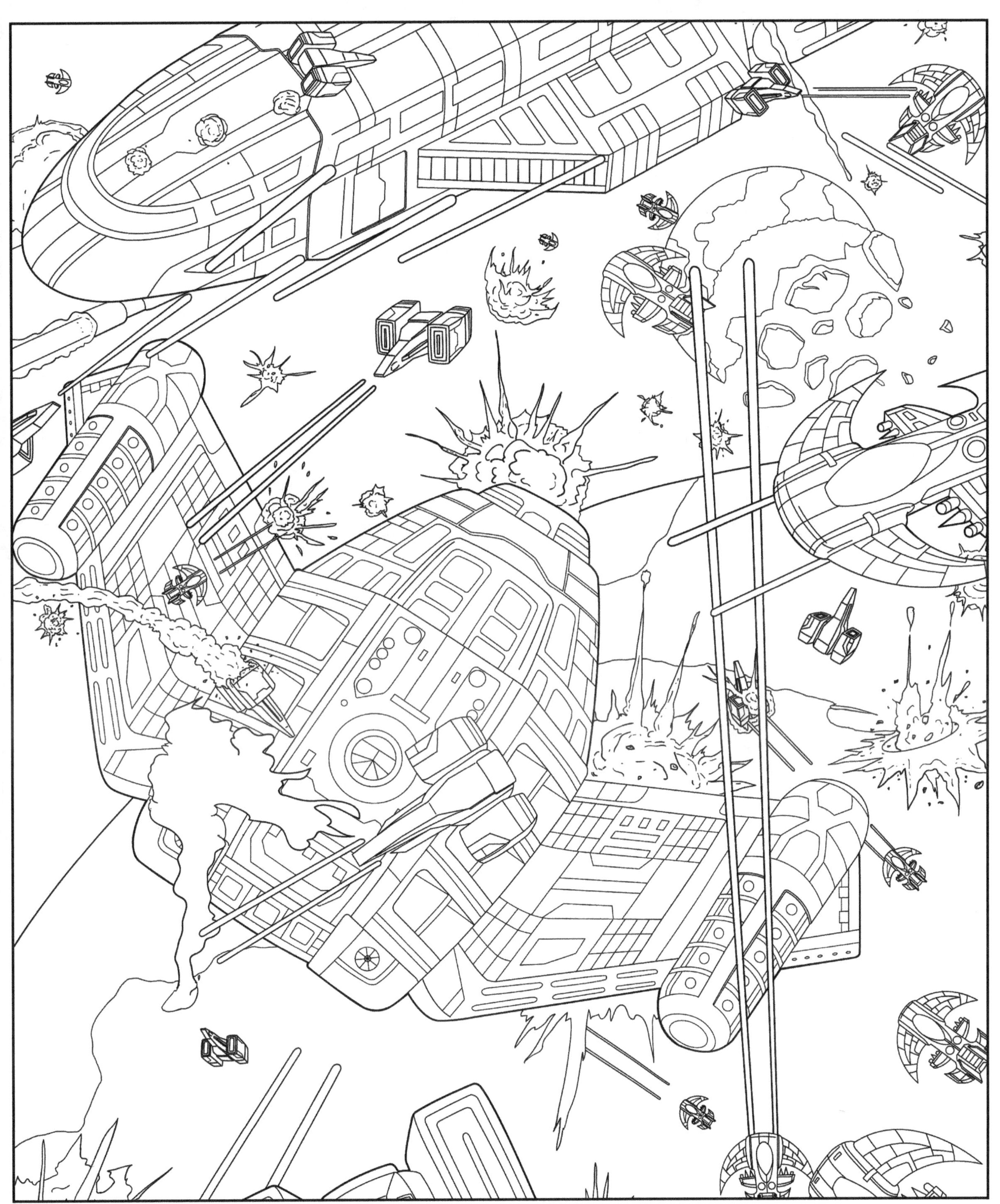

The company, Friendly Corp, uses its army to attack human settlements in deep space to claim their territory.

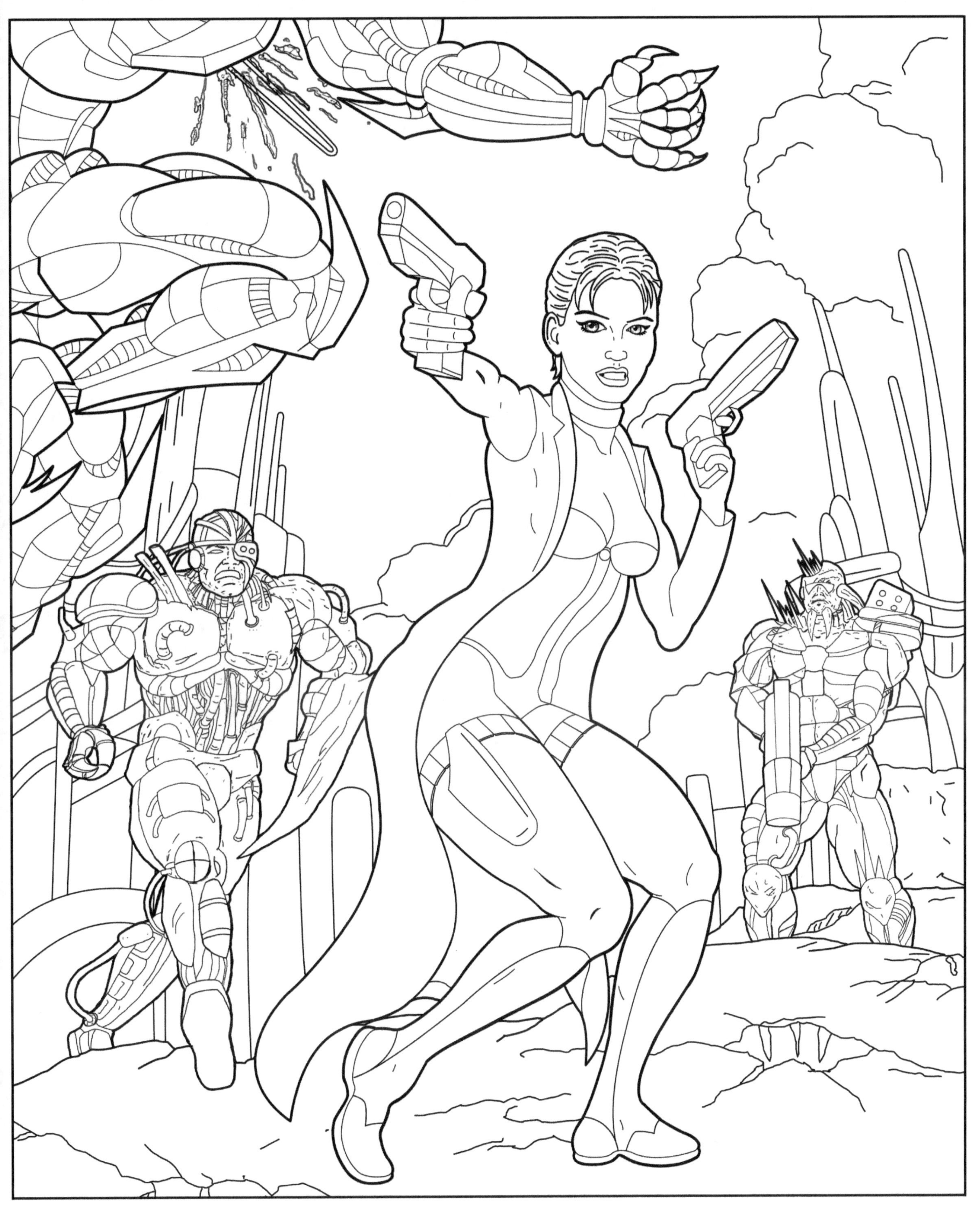

Sage fends off an attack by cyborg members of the Gladiator Gang!

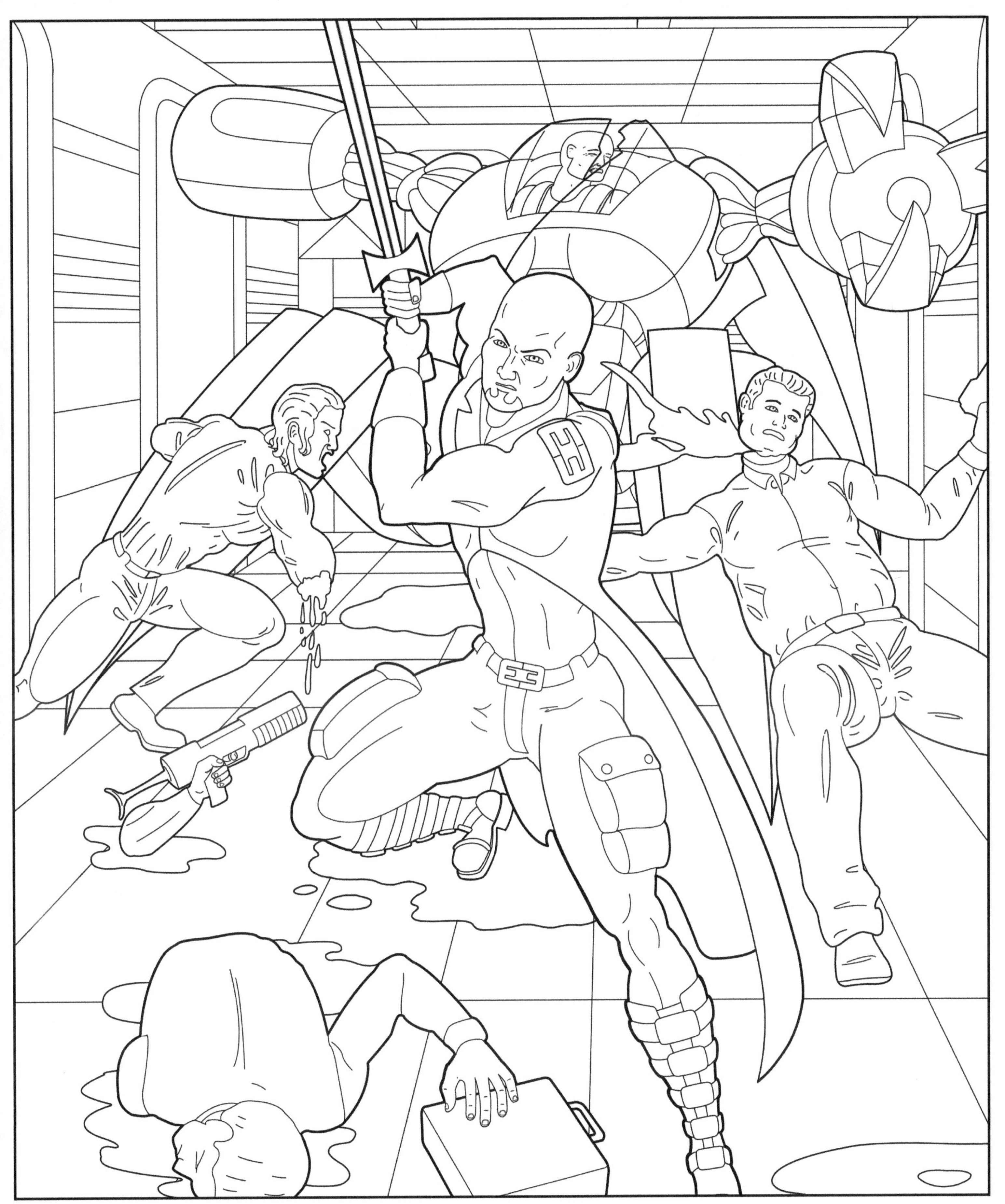

John Nihil was upgraded to become a puppet of
Friendly Corp, but he managed to escape.

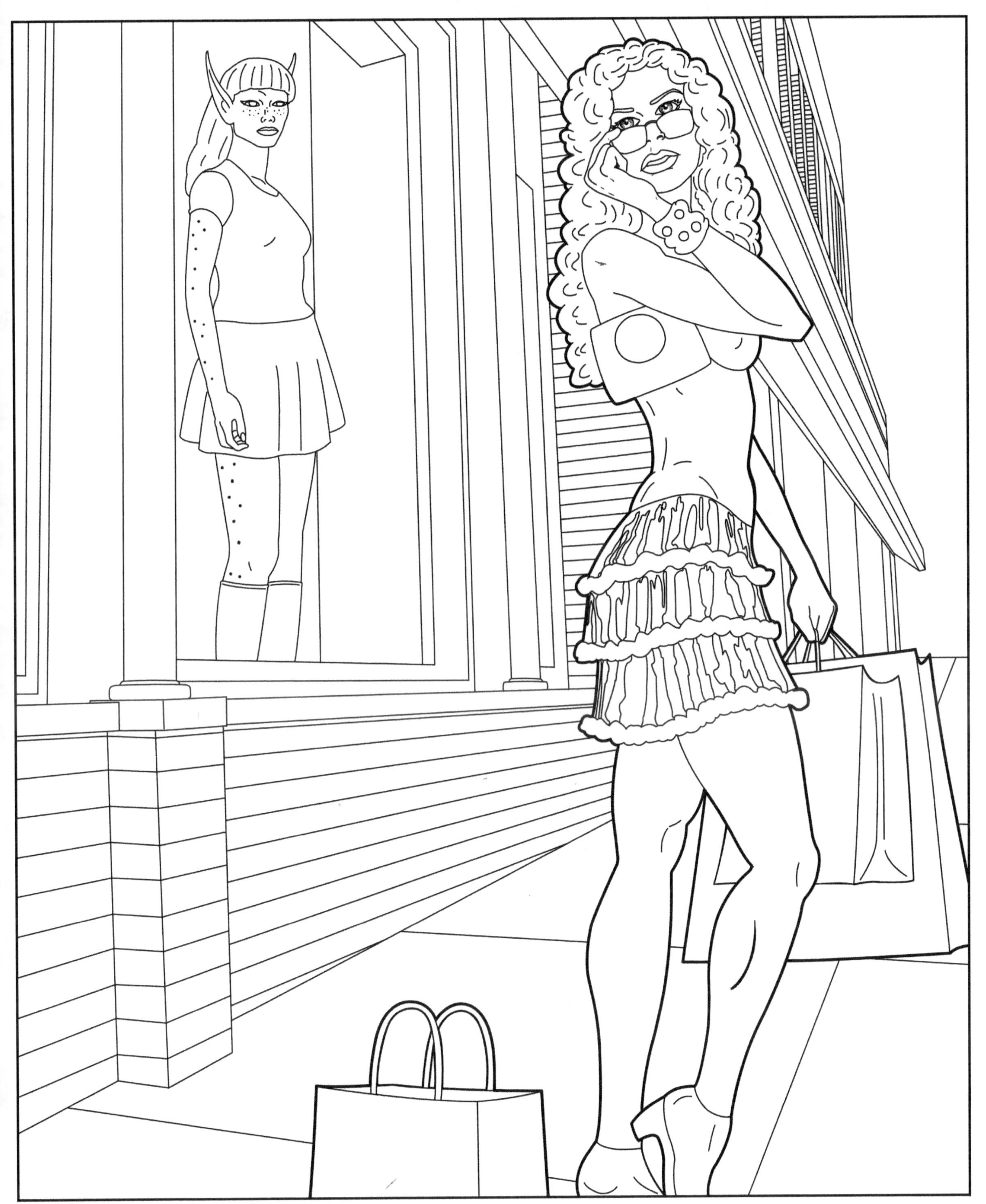

Imogen is heiress to a great fortune, and has family ties to Friendly Corp.

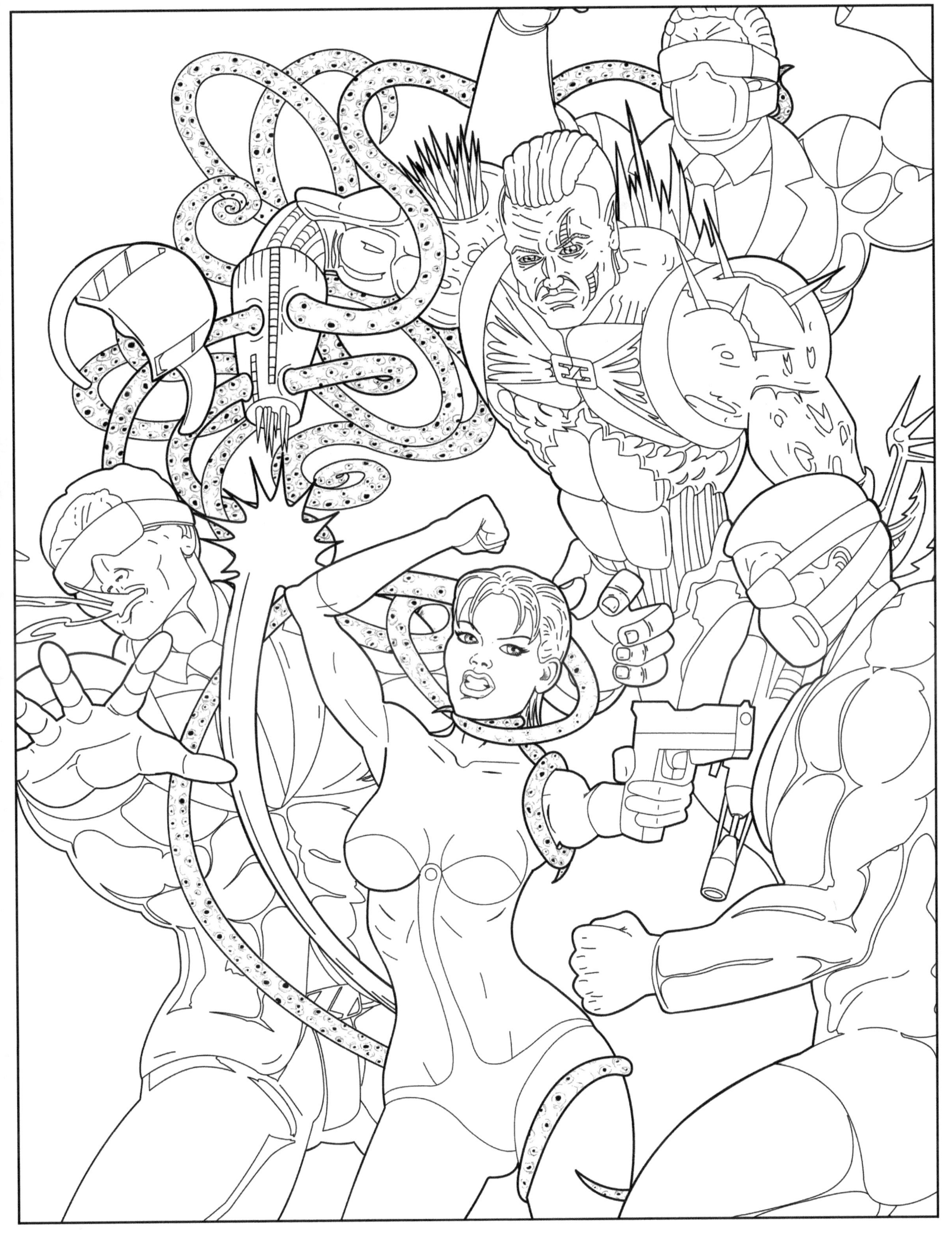

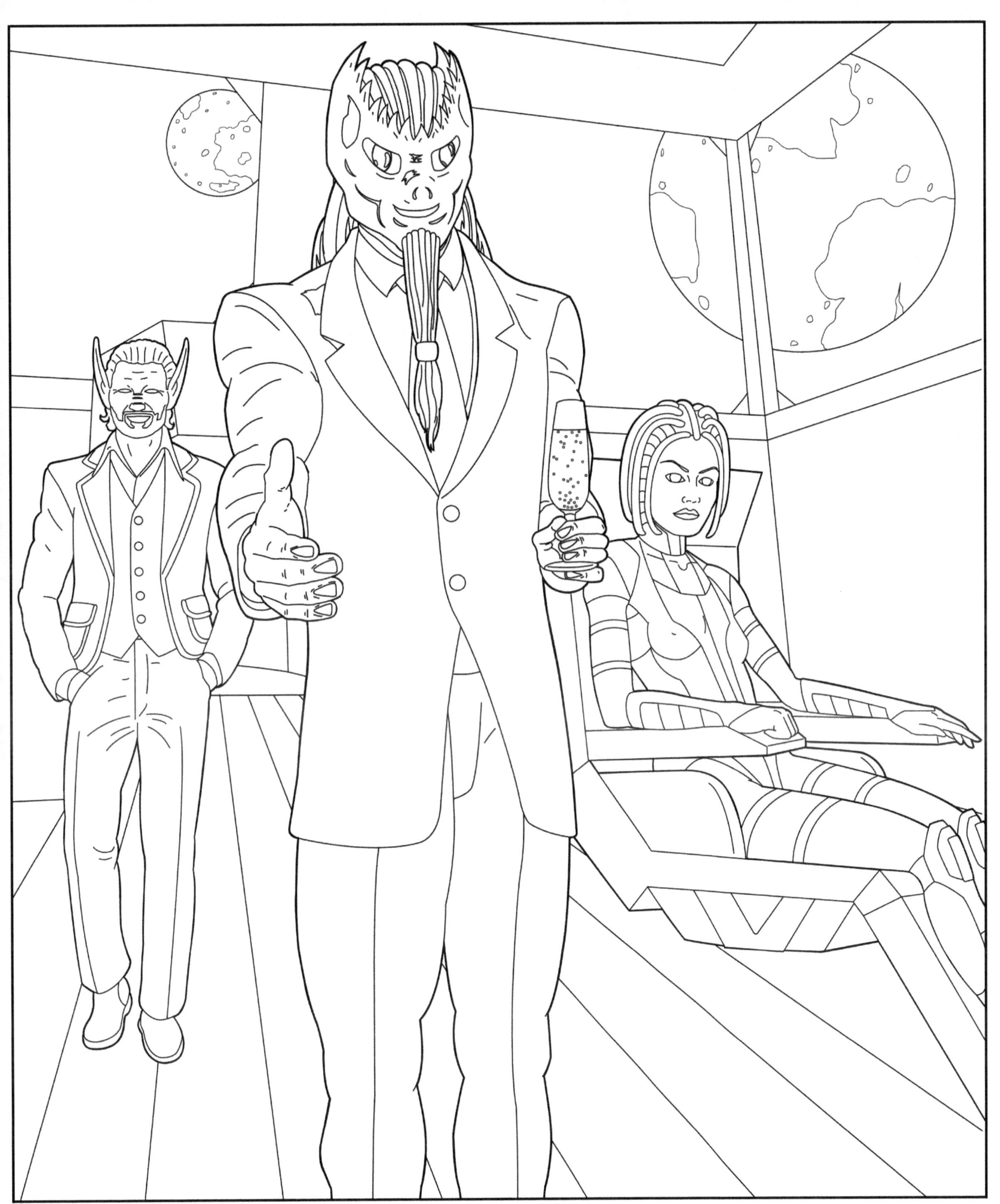

Doctor Barazil, council member Adruh, and engineer Hess meet with diplomats on a remote space station.

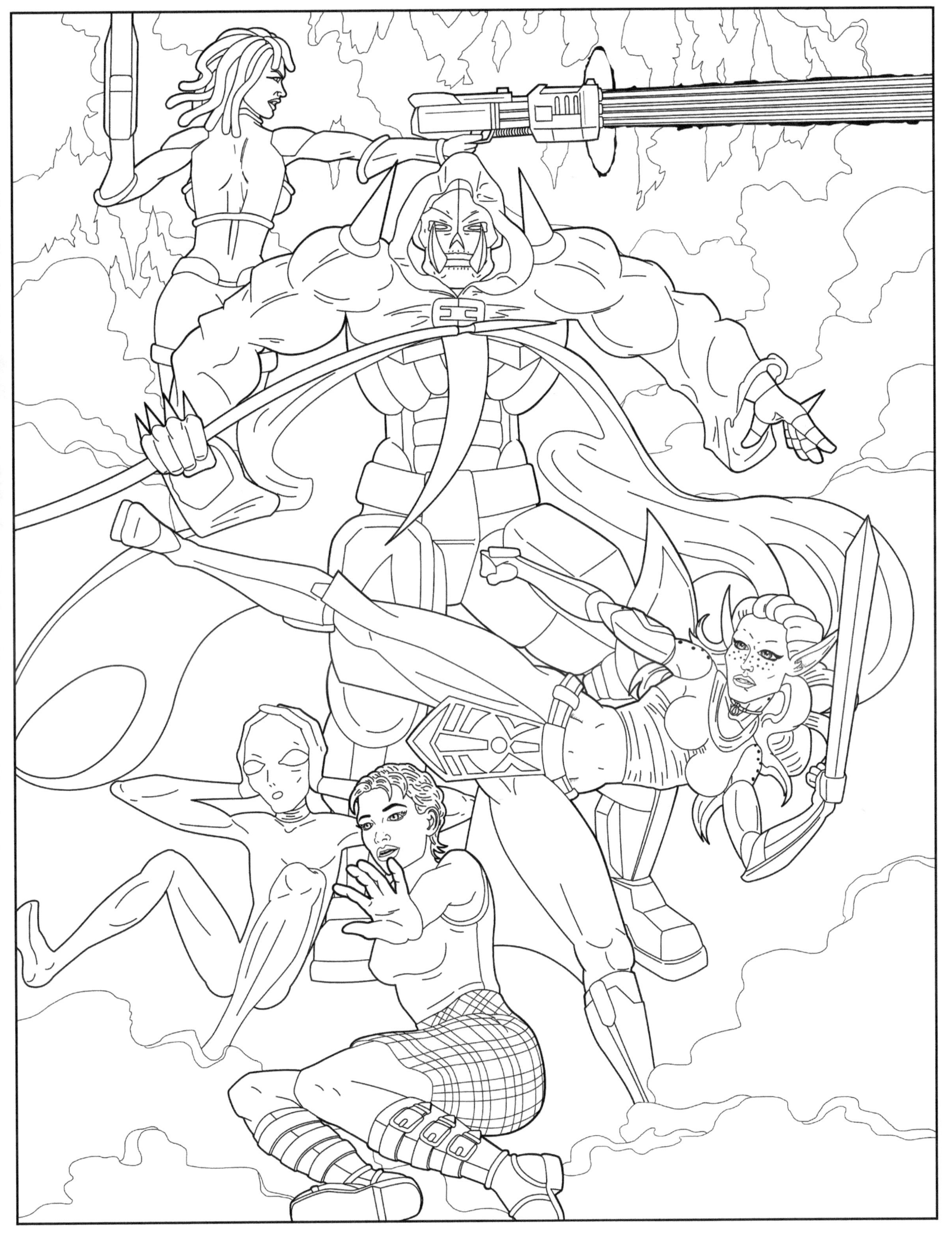

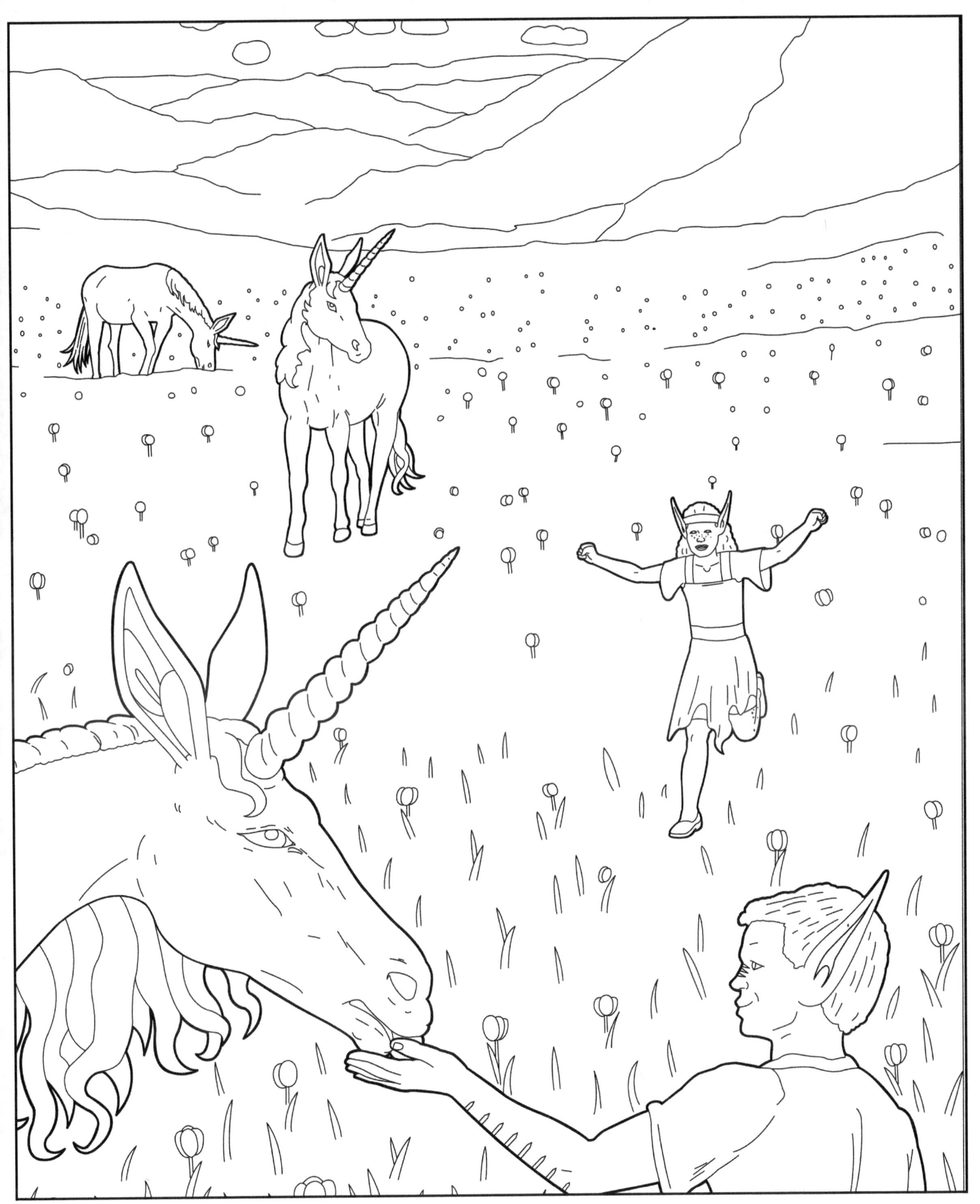

Perian Prime is the home world of the Perian race, and has native unicorns.

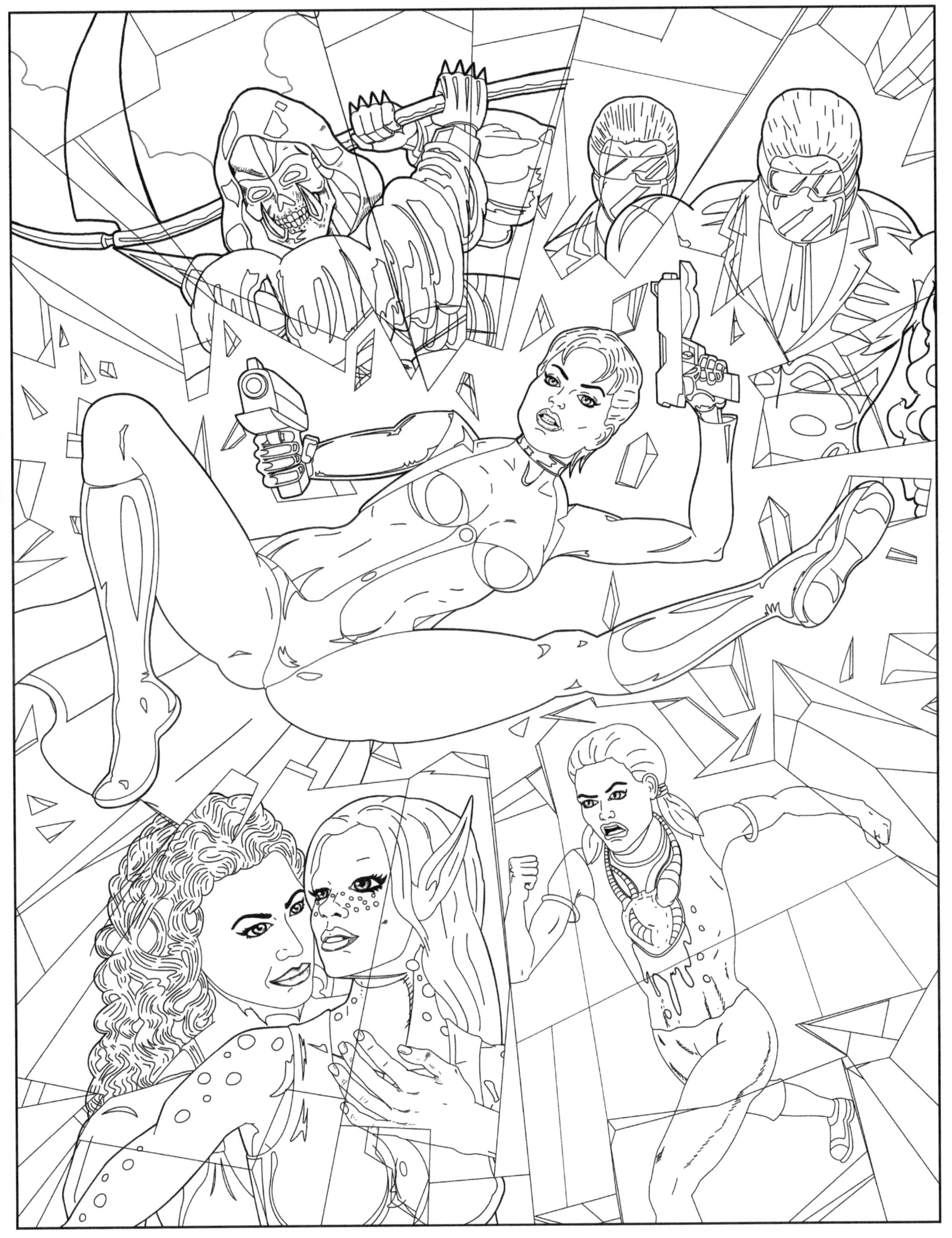

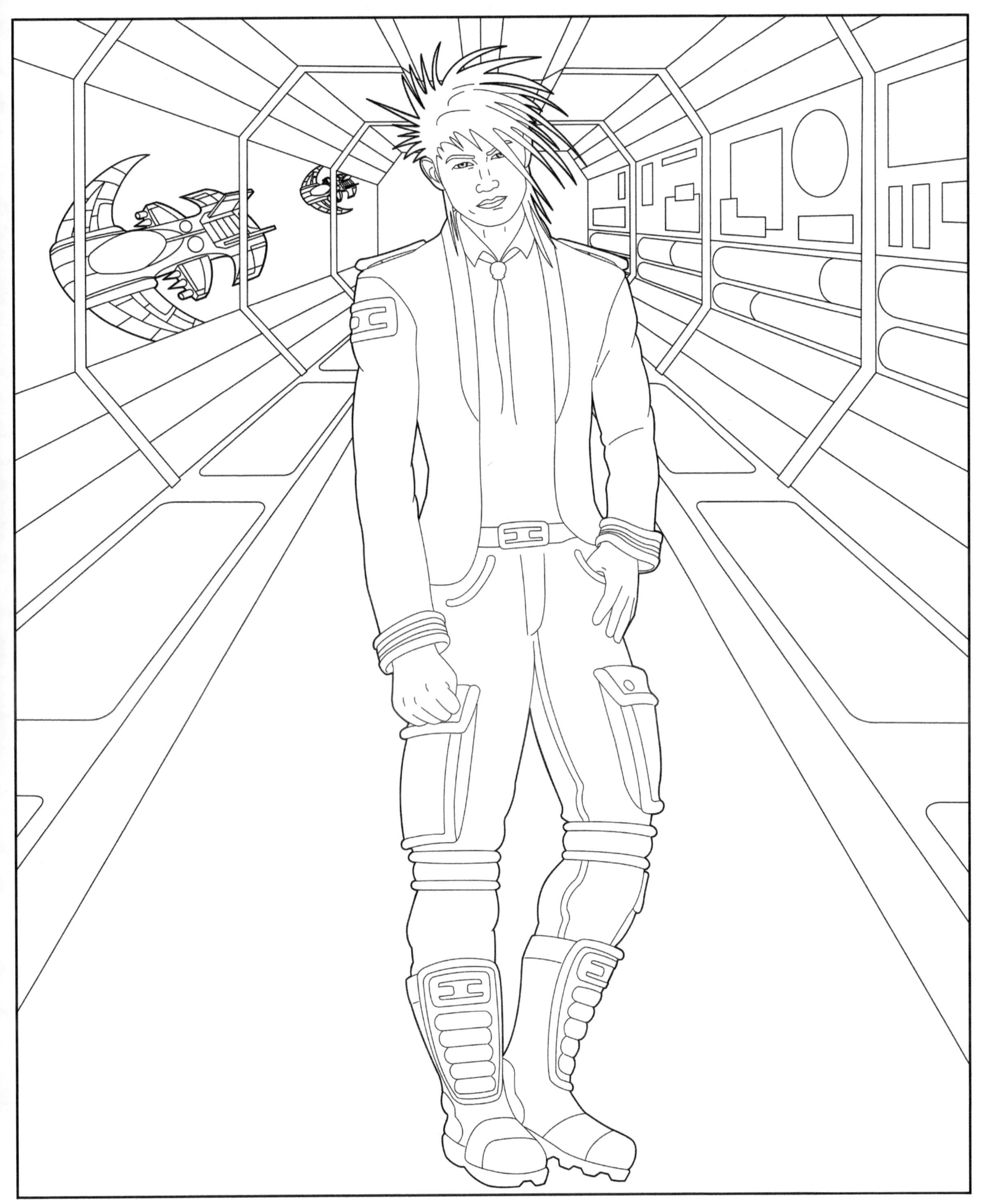

Salesman Assassin, Karma, can absorb energy and redirect it.

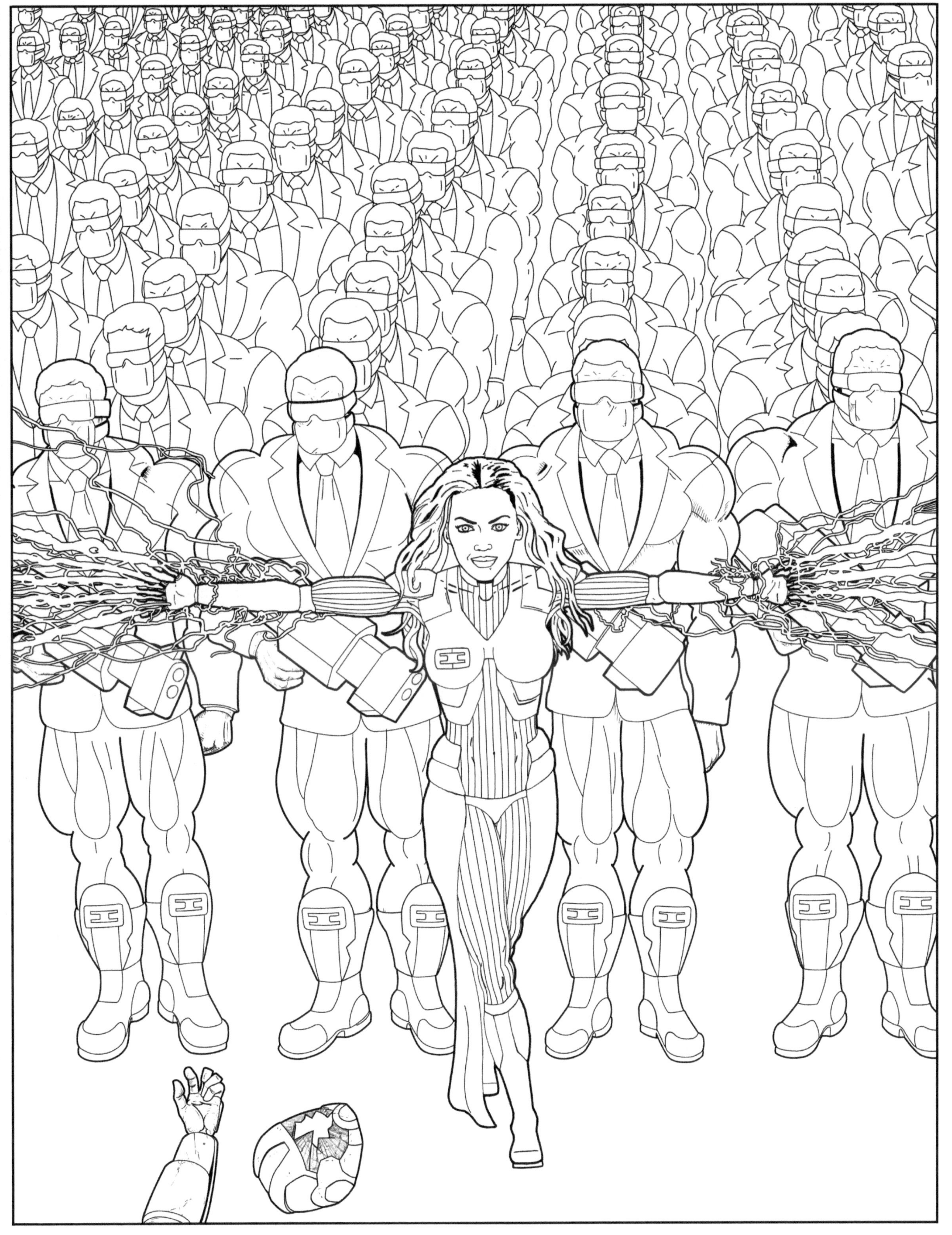

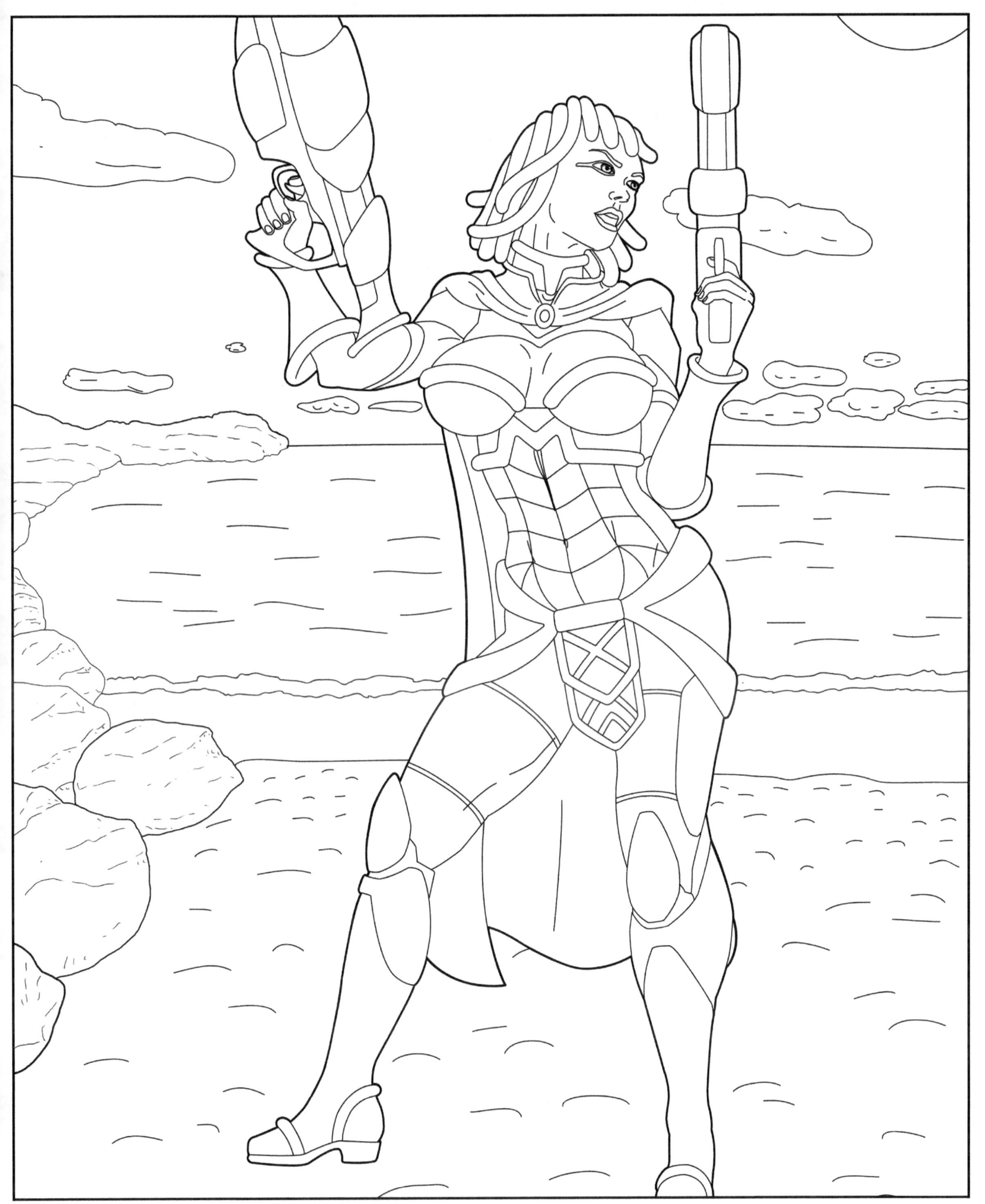

Vidatha comes from a female warrior race. She is experienced and headstrong.

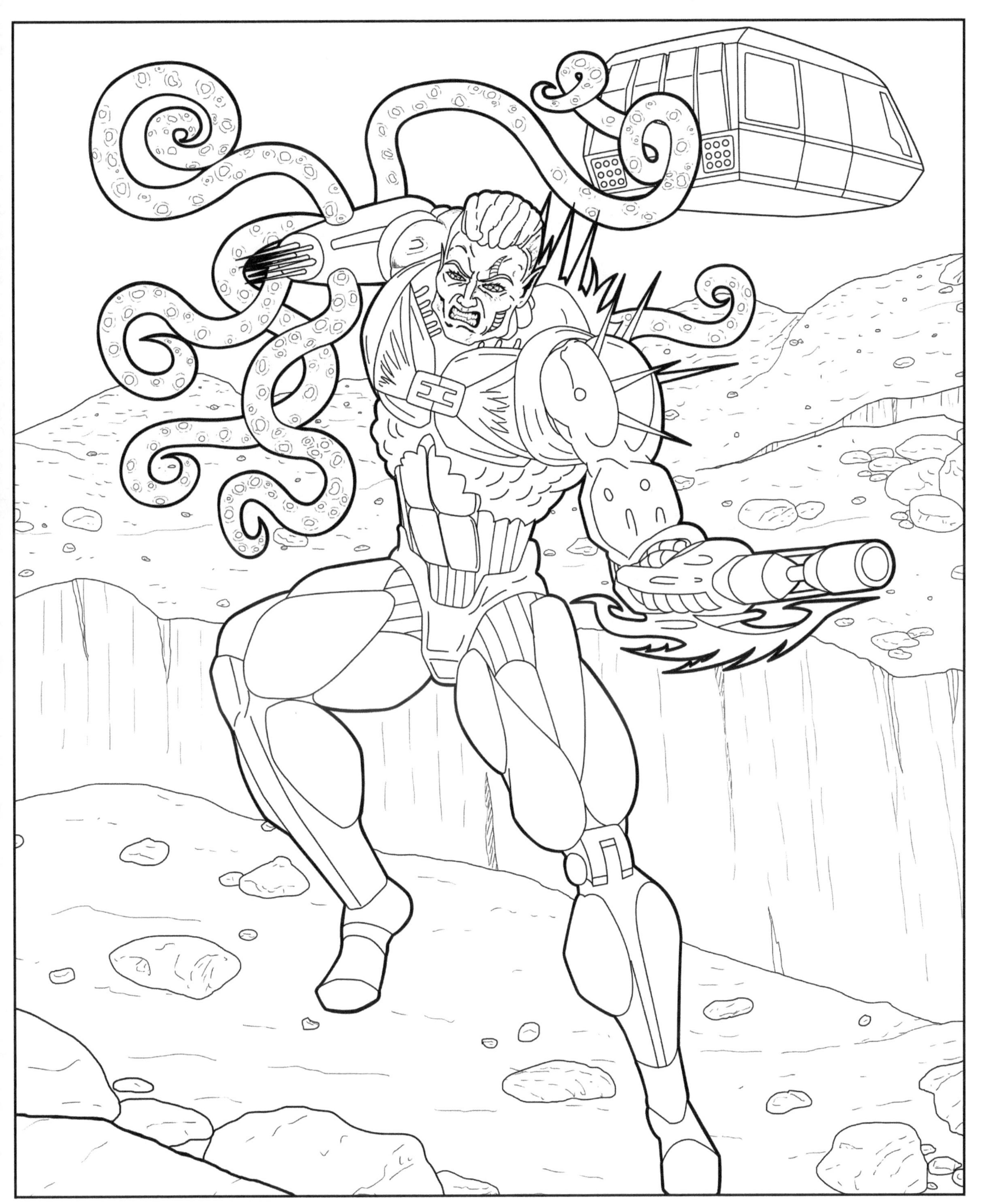

Groth is a former Salesman Assassin turned bounty hunter.

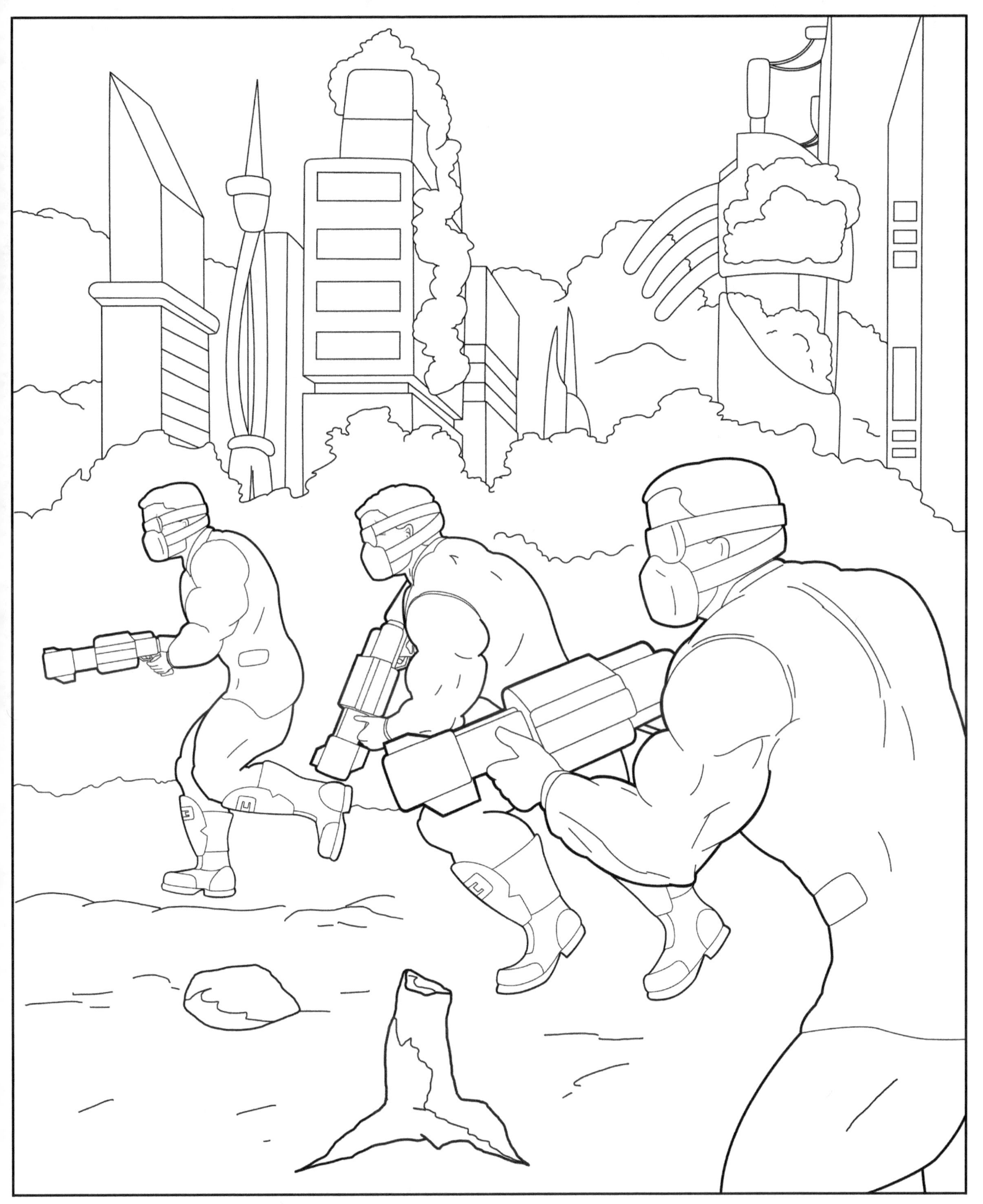

Level 6 Salesman Assassins are heavy-duty warriors who think with a hive mind.

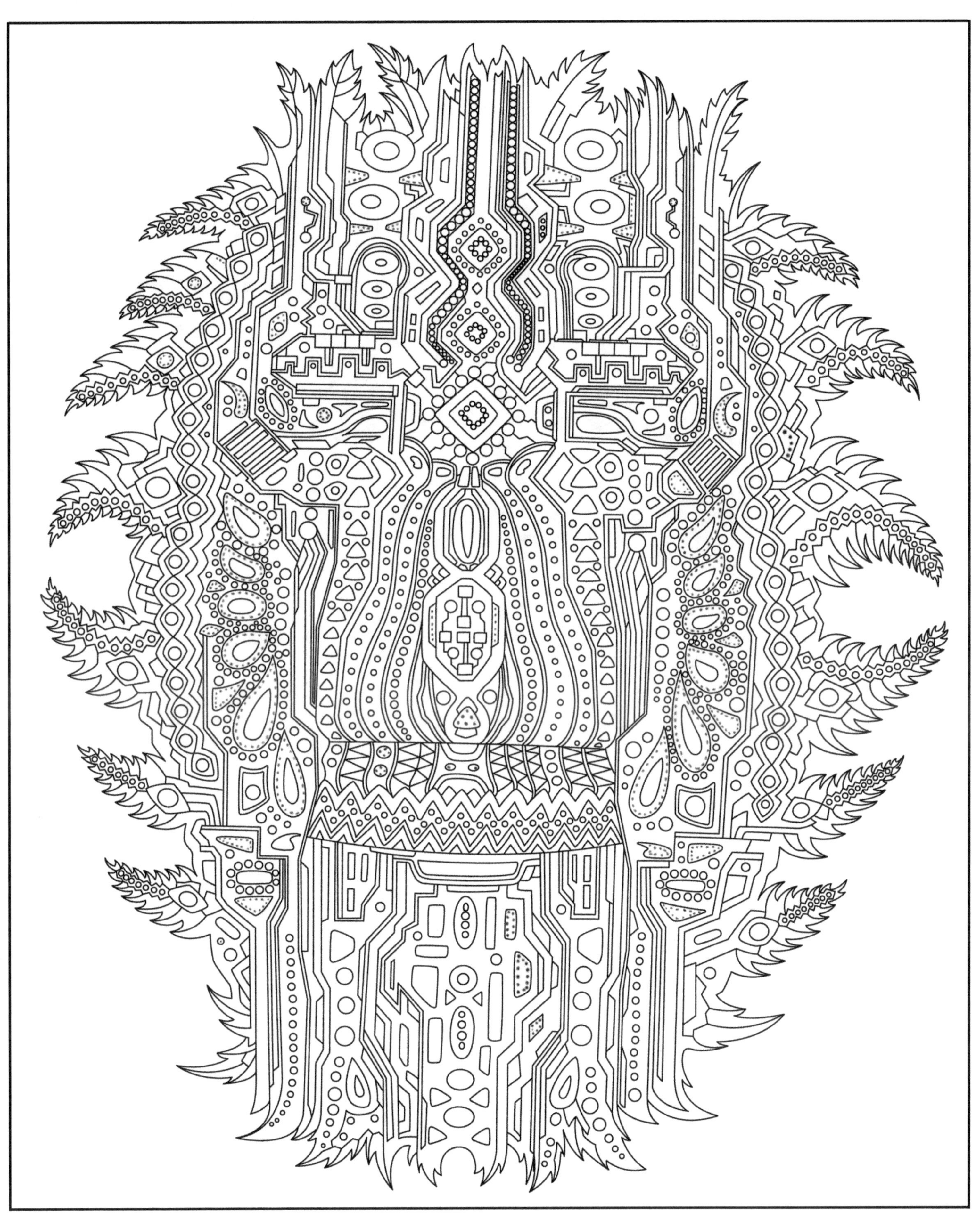

The universal mind Grim witnessed when he travelled back through space and time.

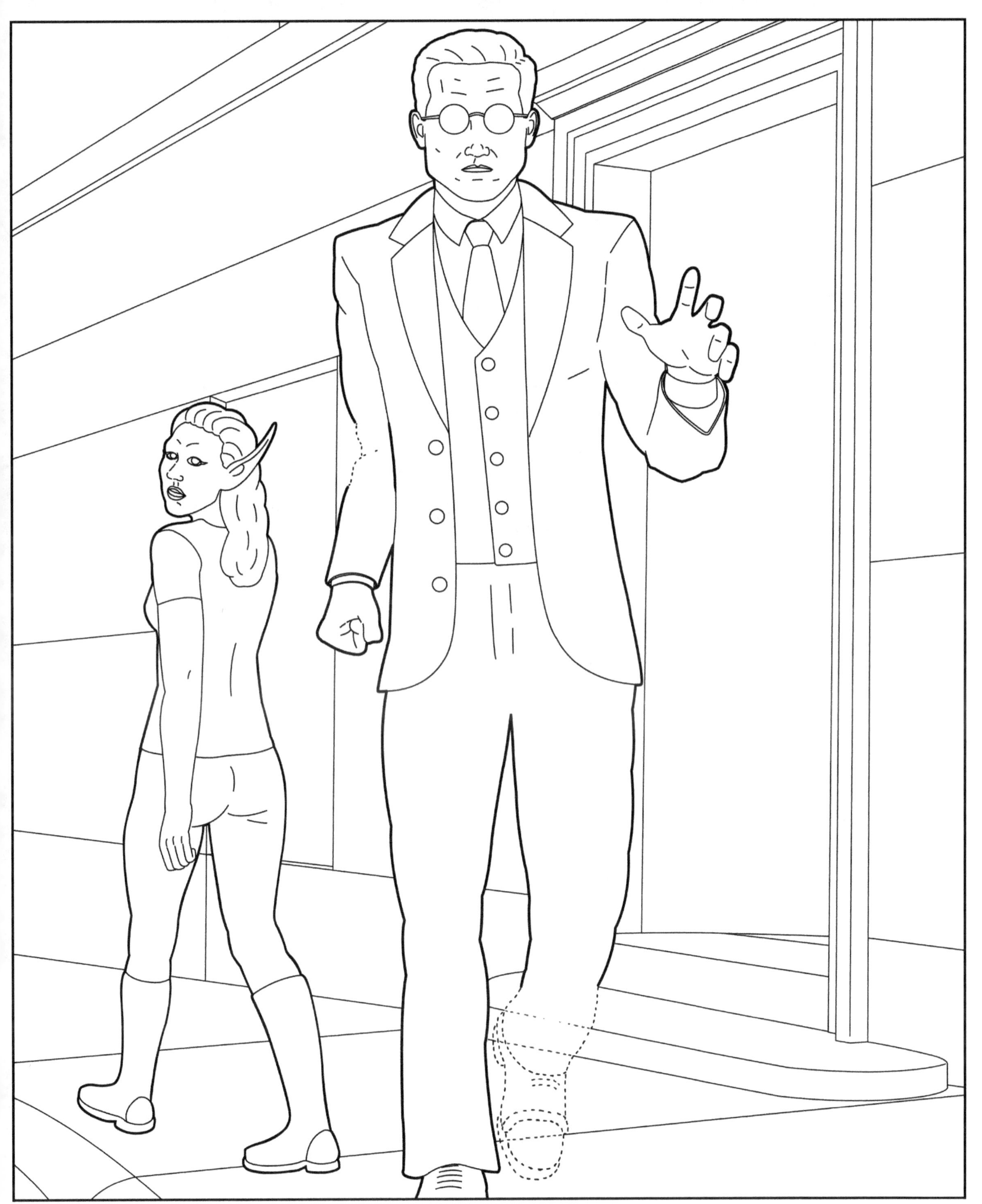

The entity known as The Final Word can walk in and out of our reality.

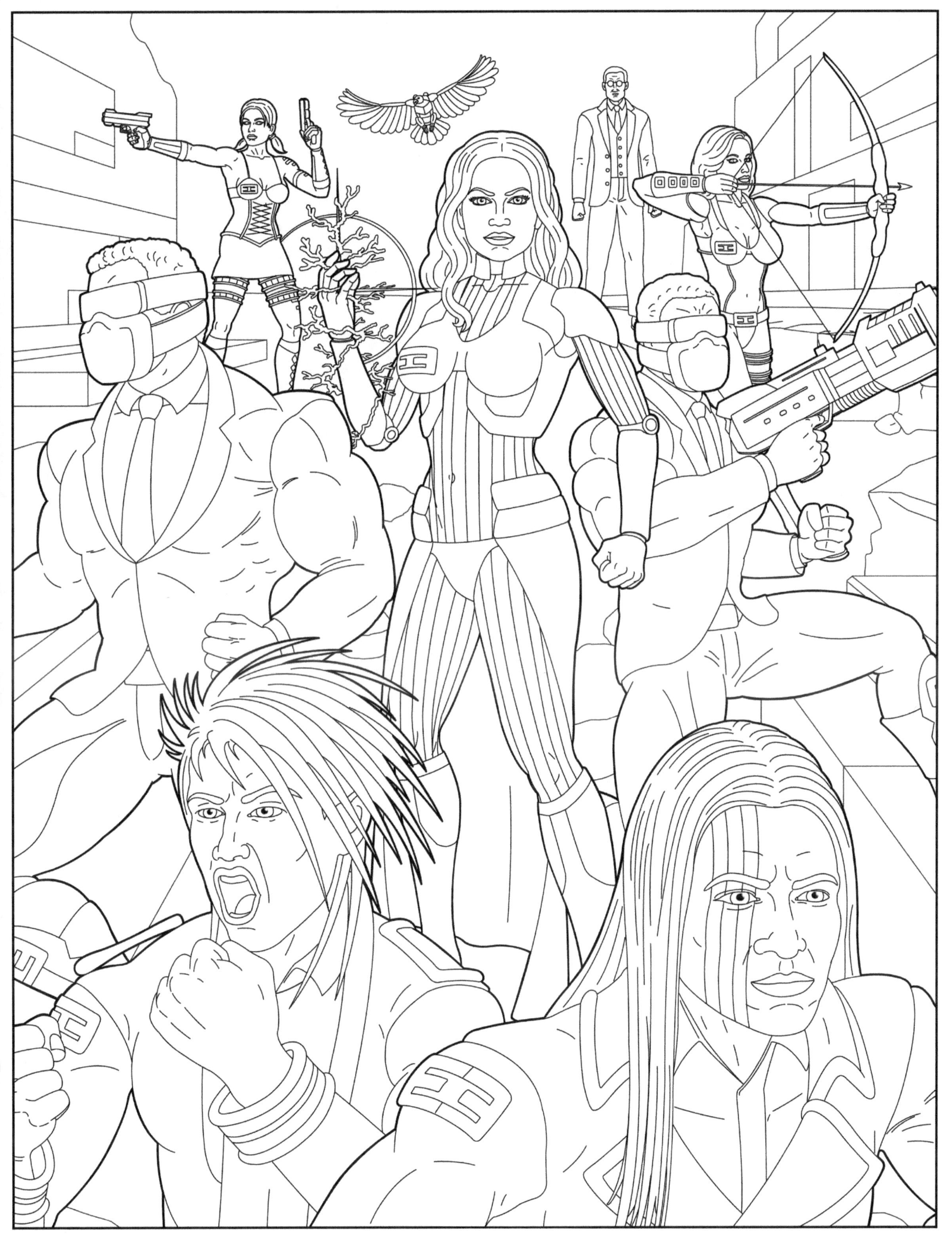

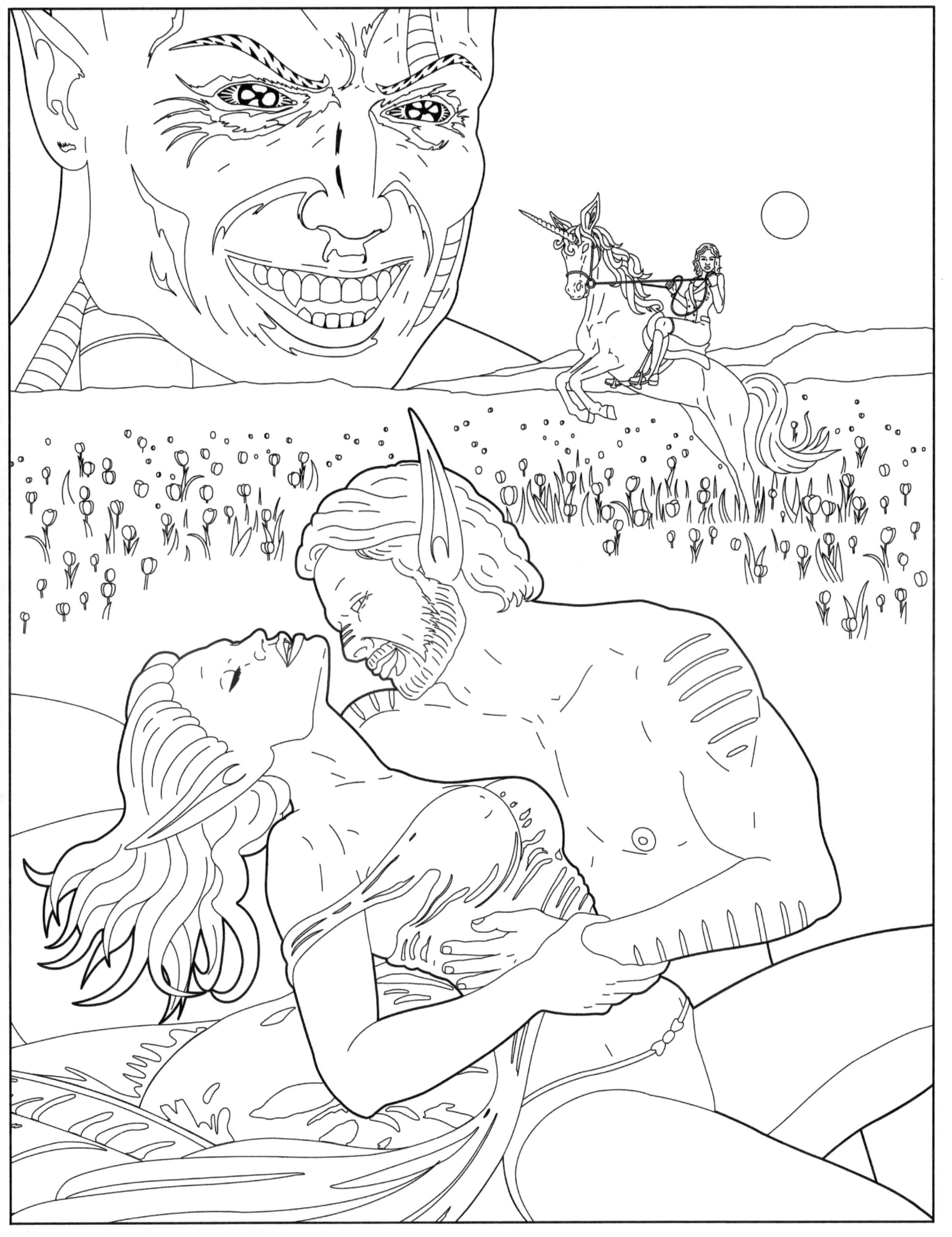

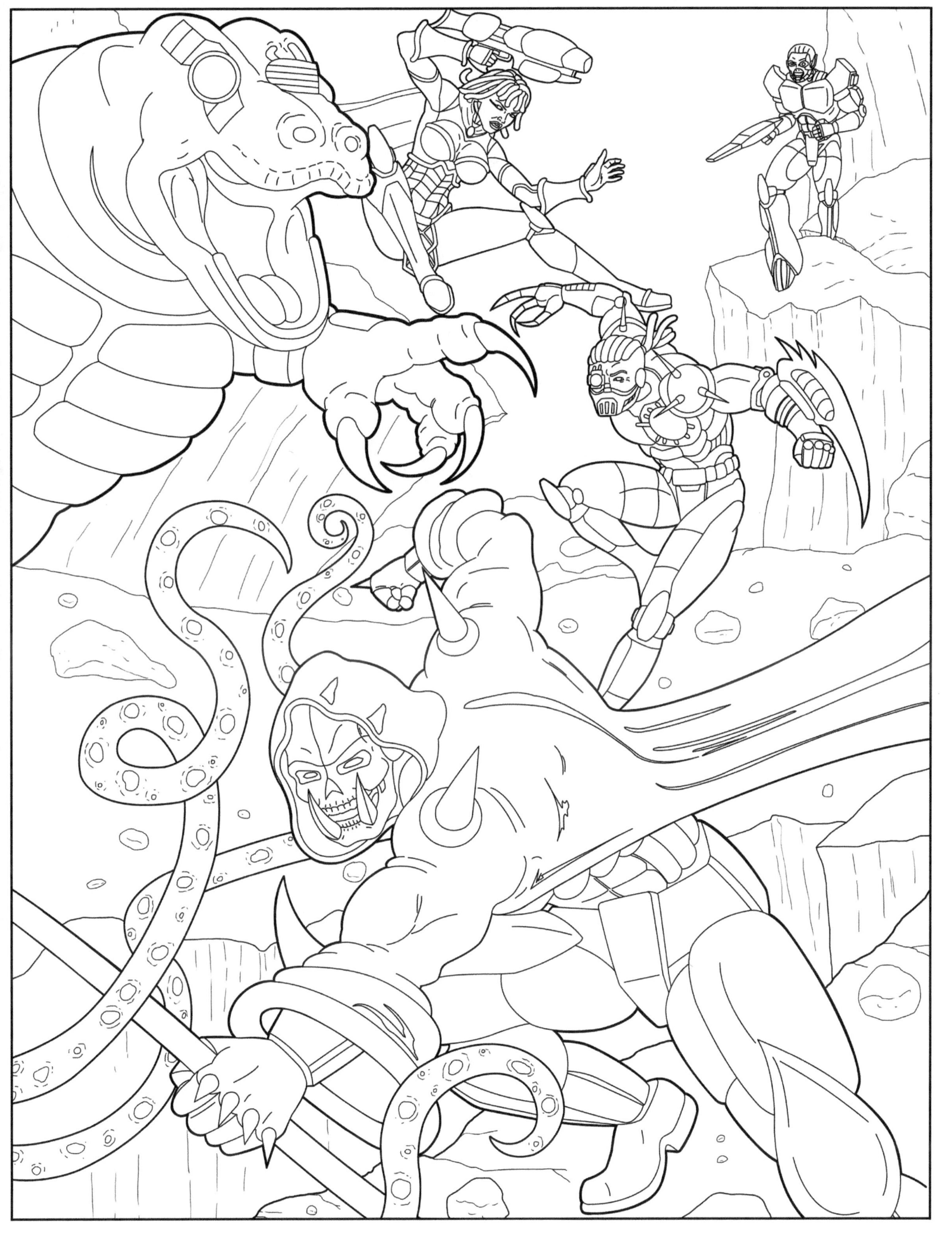

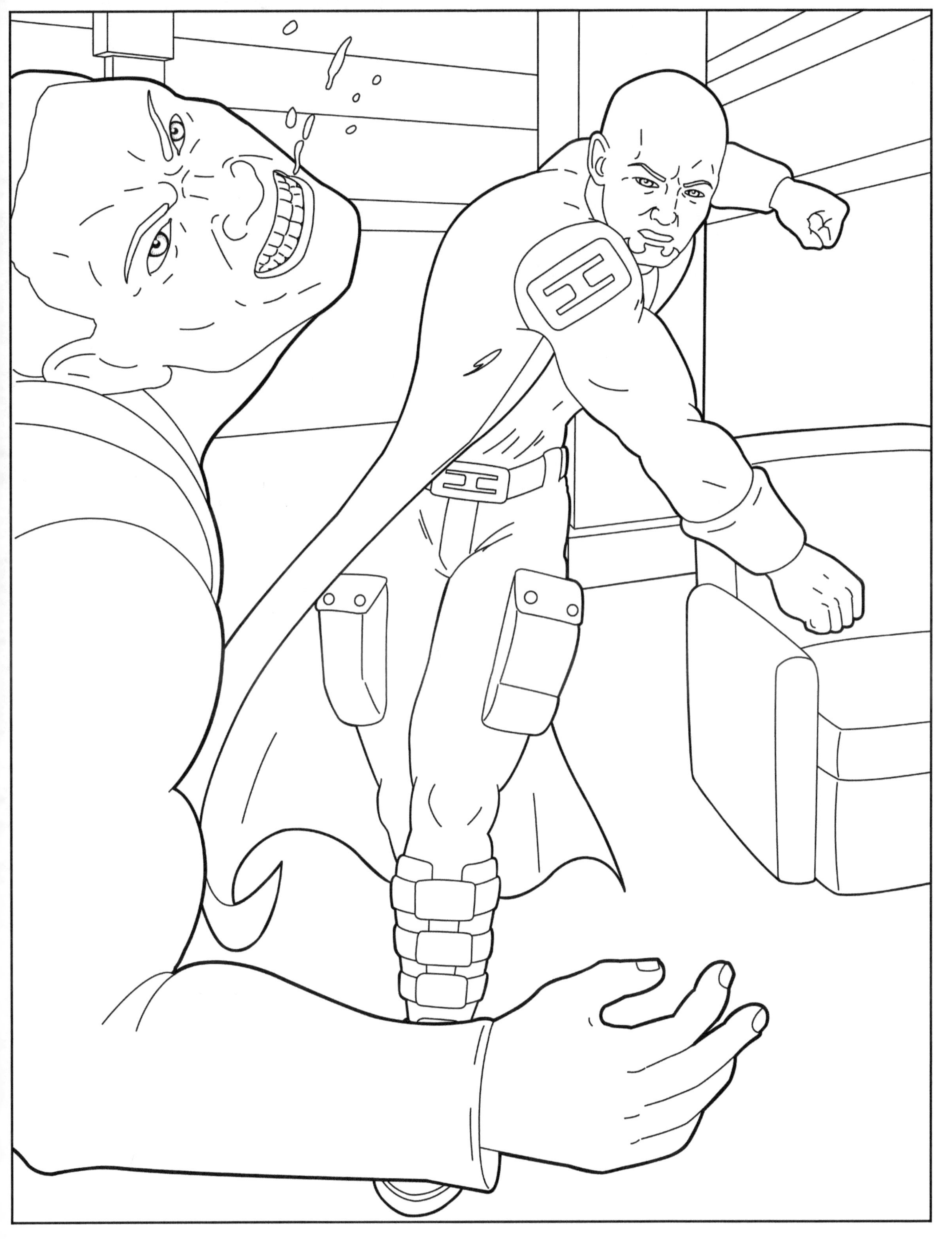

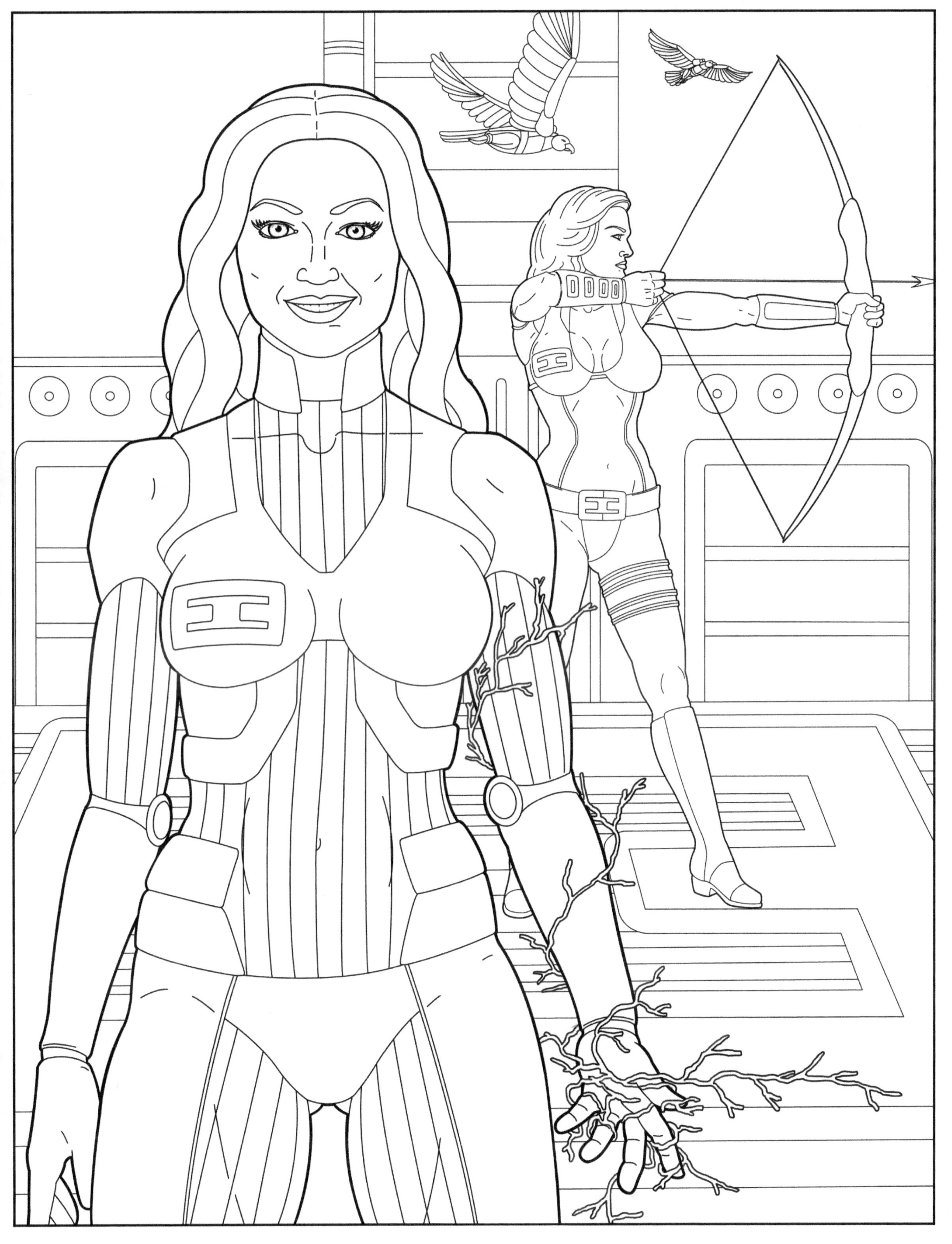

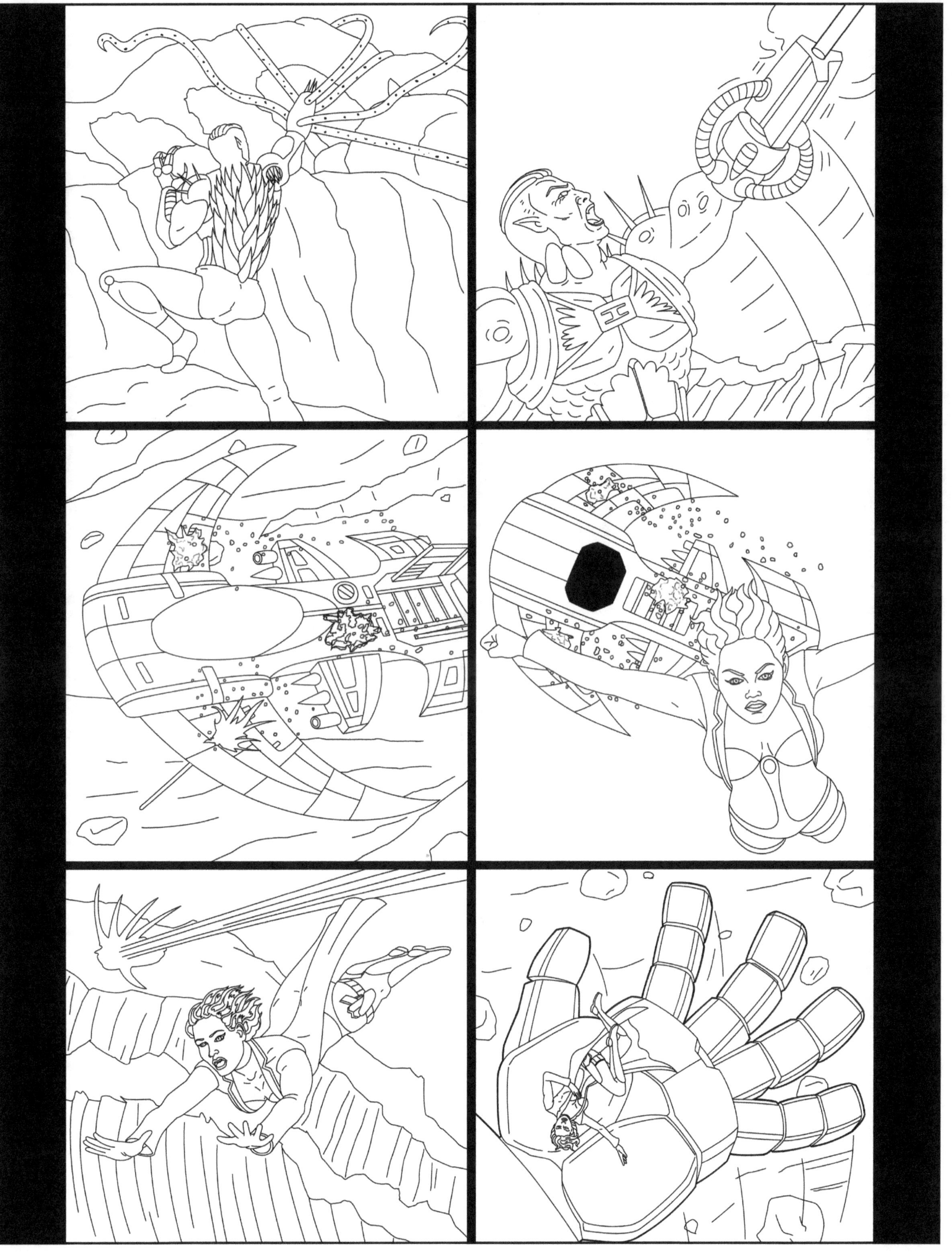

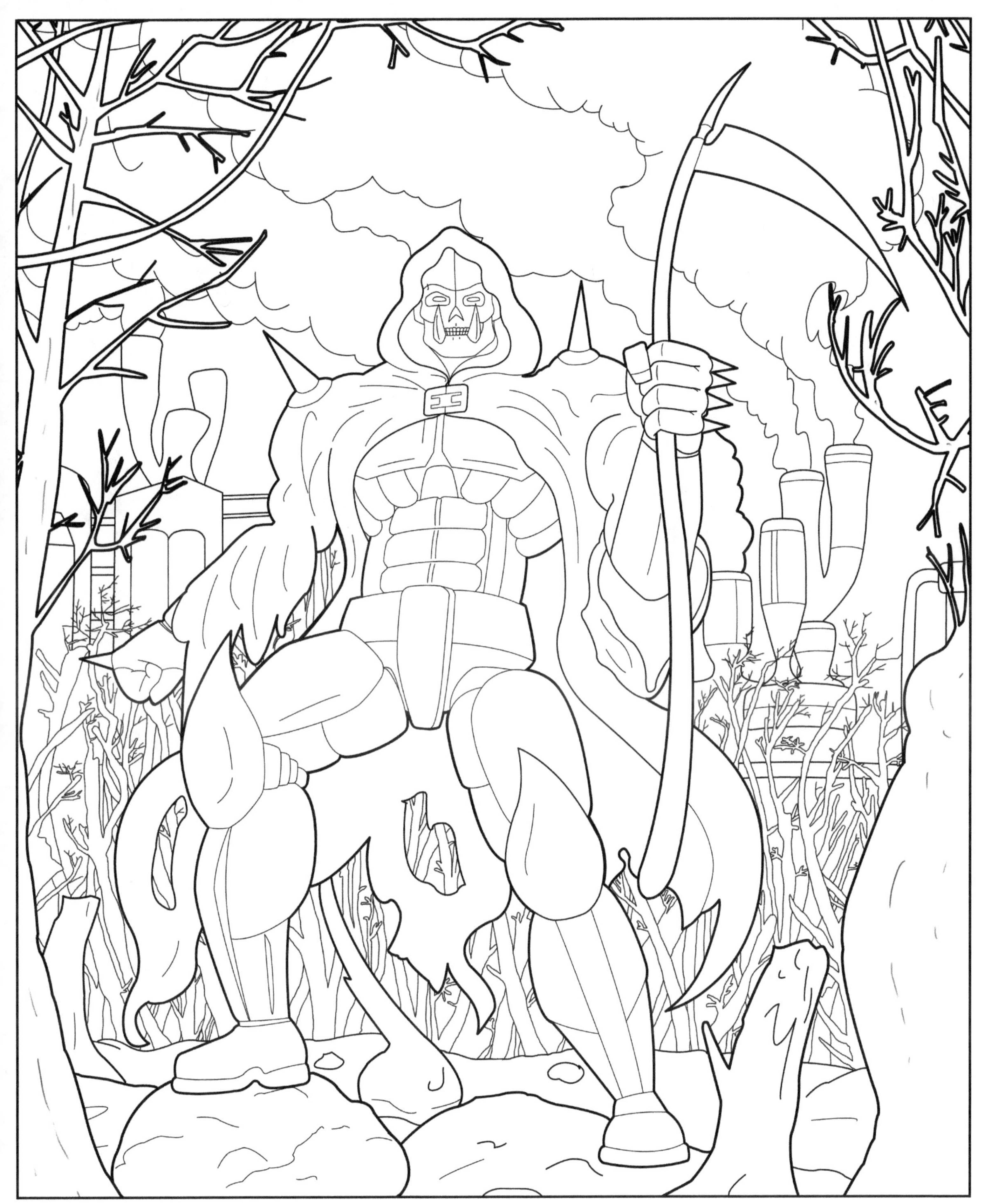

Grim is a dimension-hopping mechanoid, that has been altering our reality.

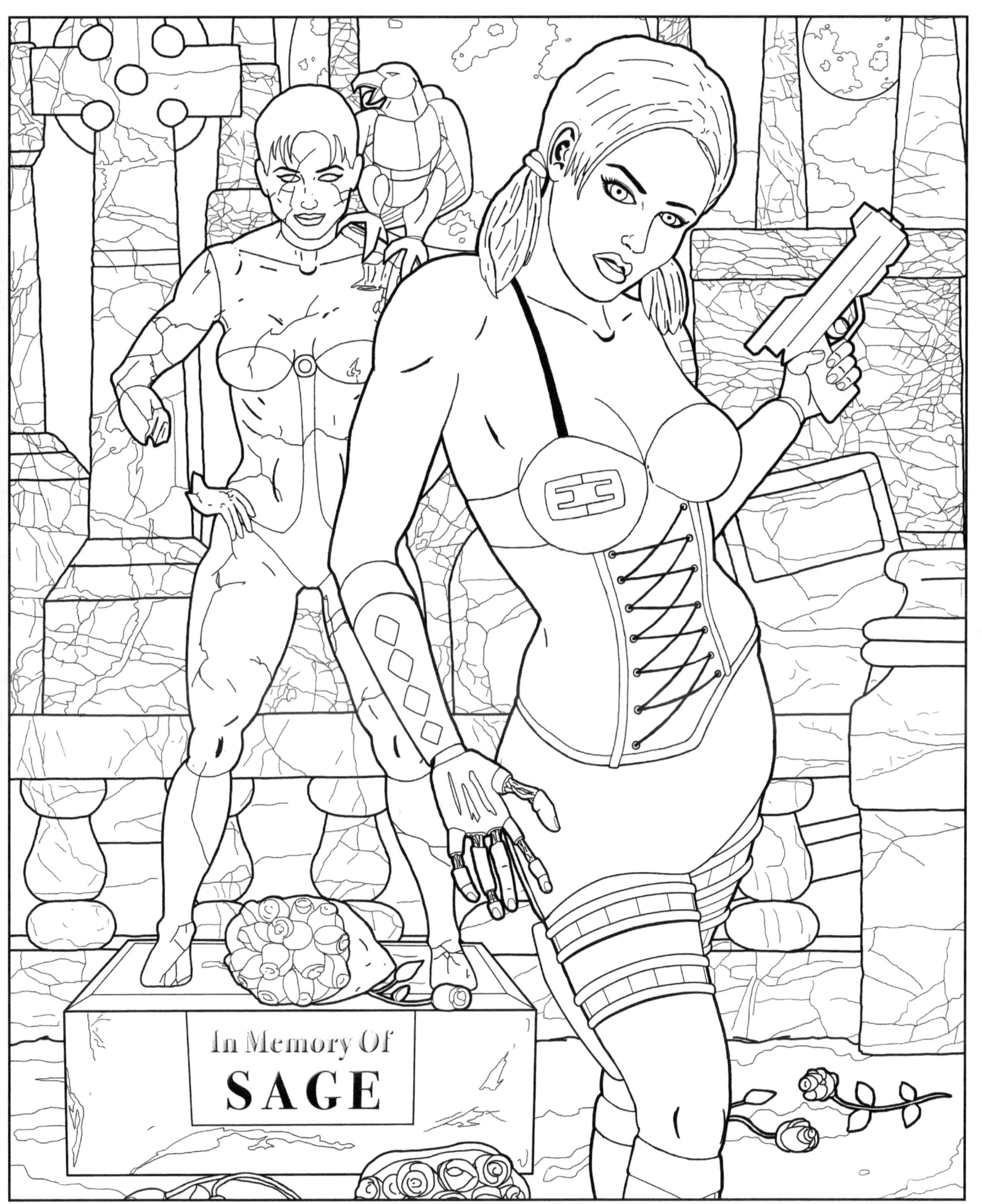

The future version of Cat has become a Salesman Assassin.

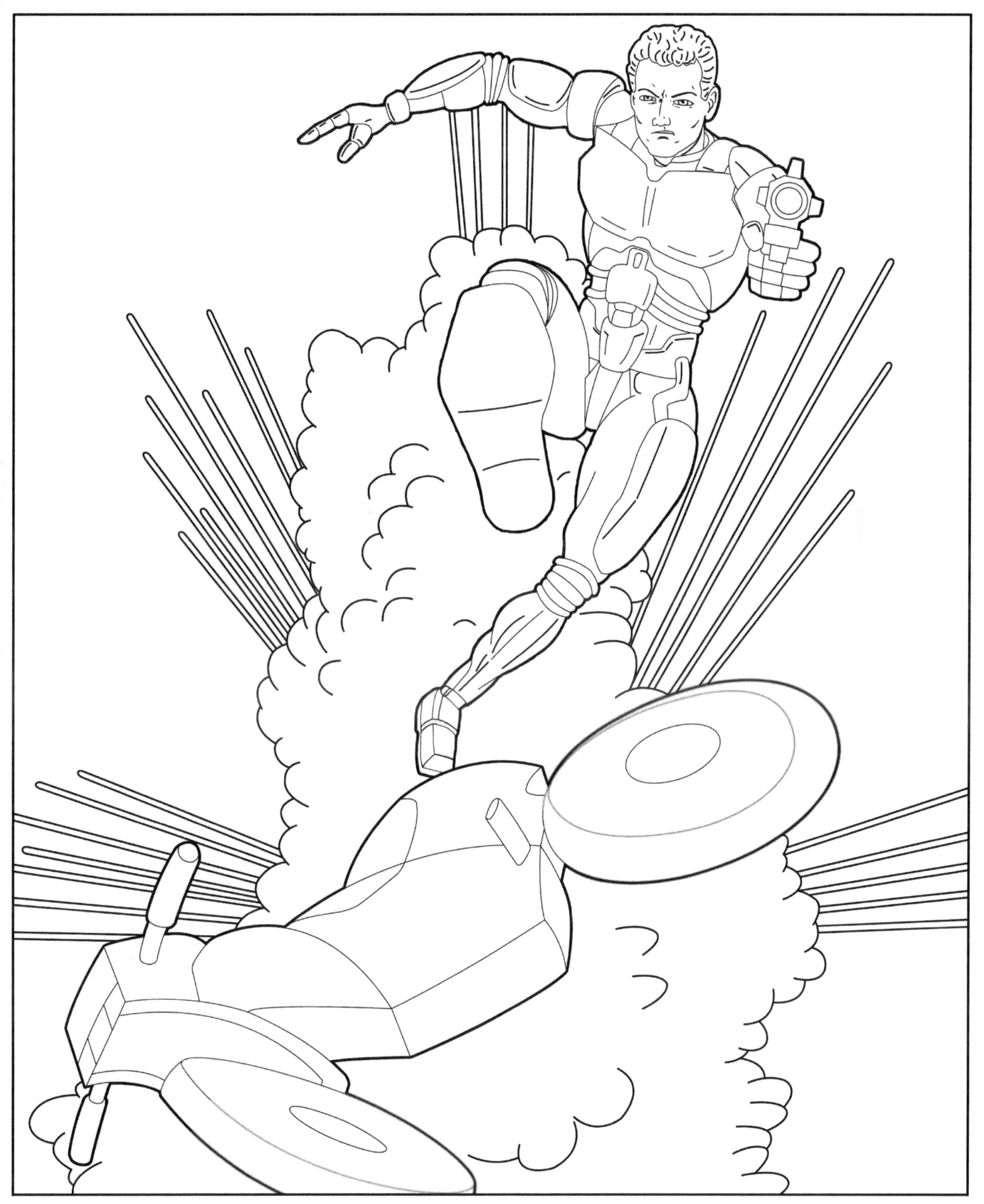

The bounty hunter Raamon leaps into action!

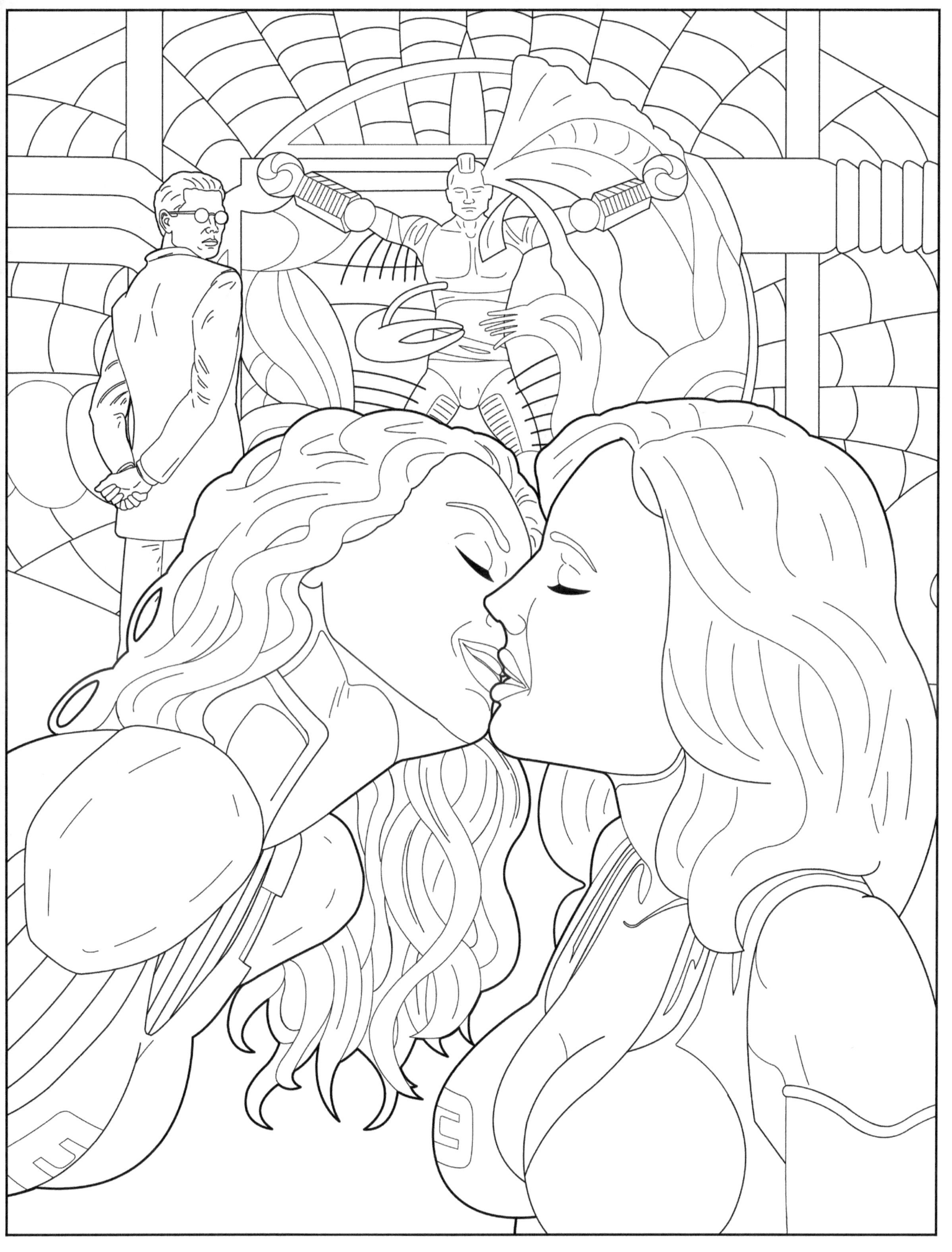

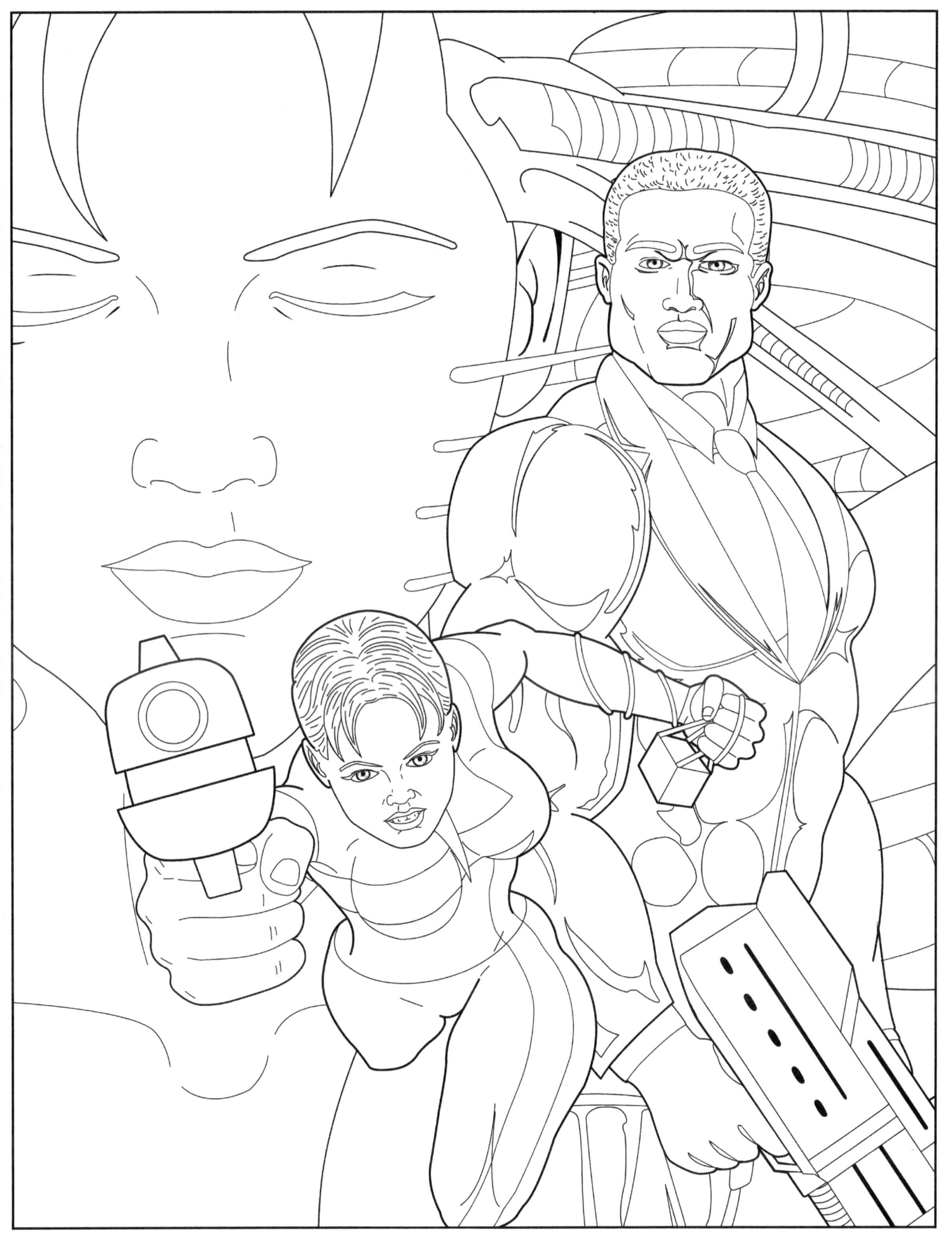

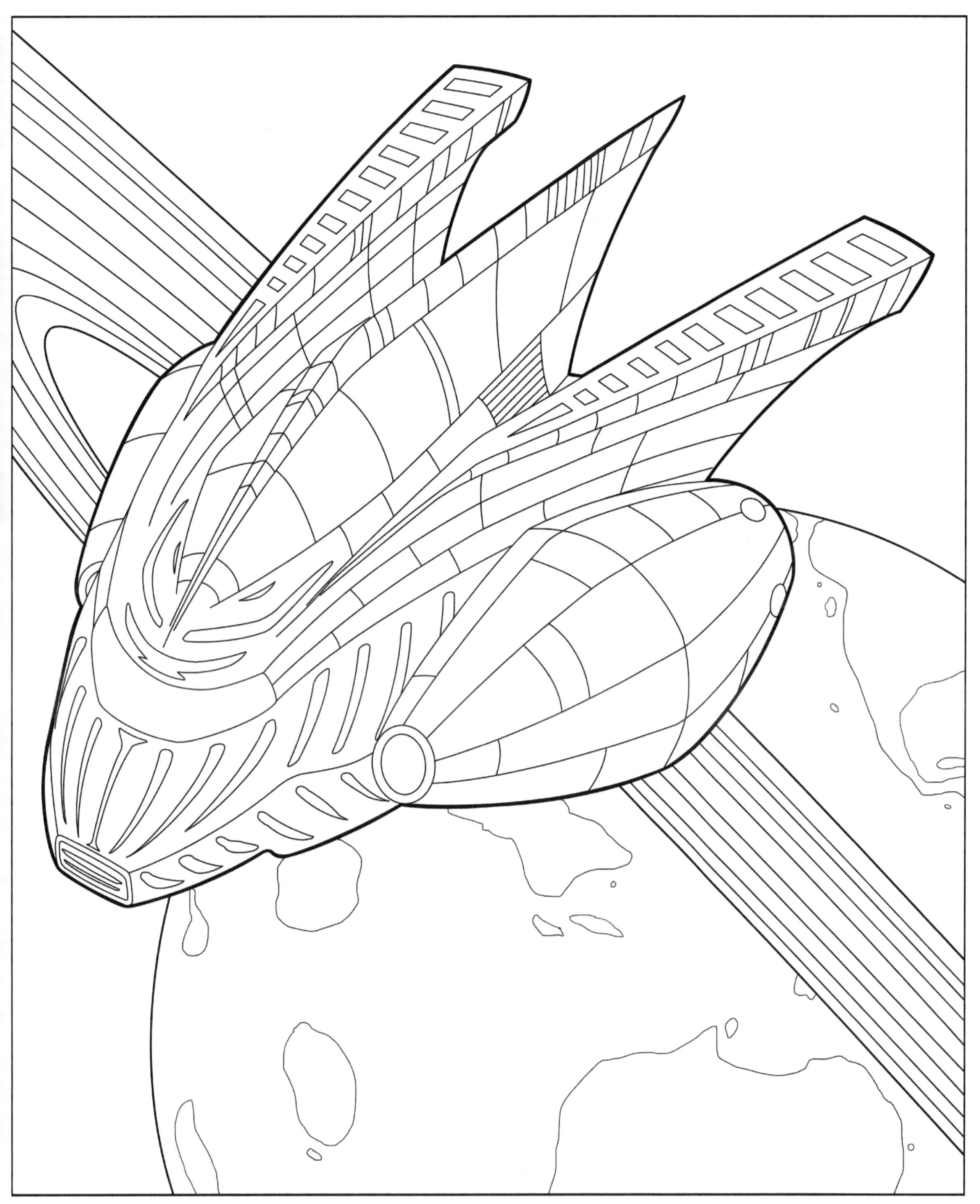

Vidatha's spaceship is called the Thantos.

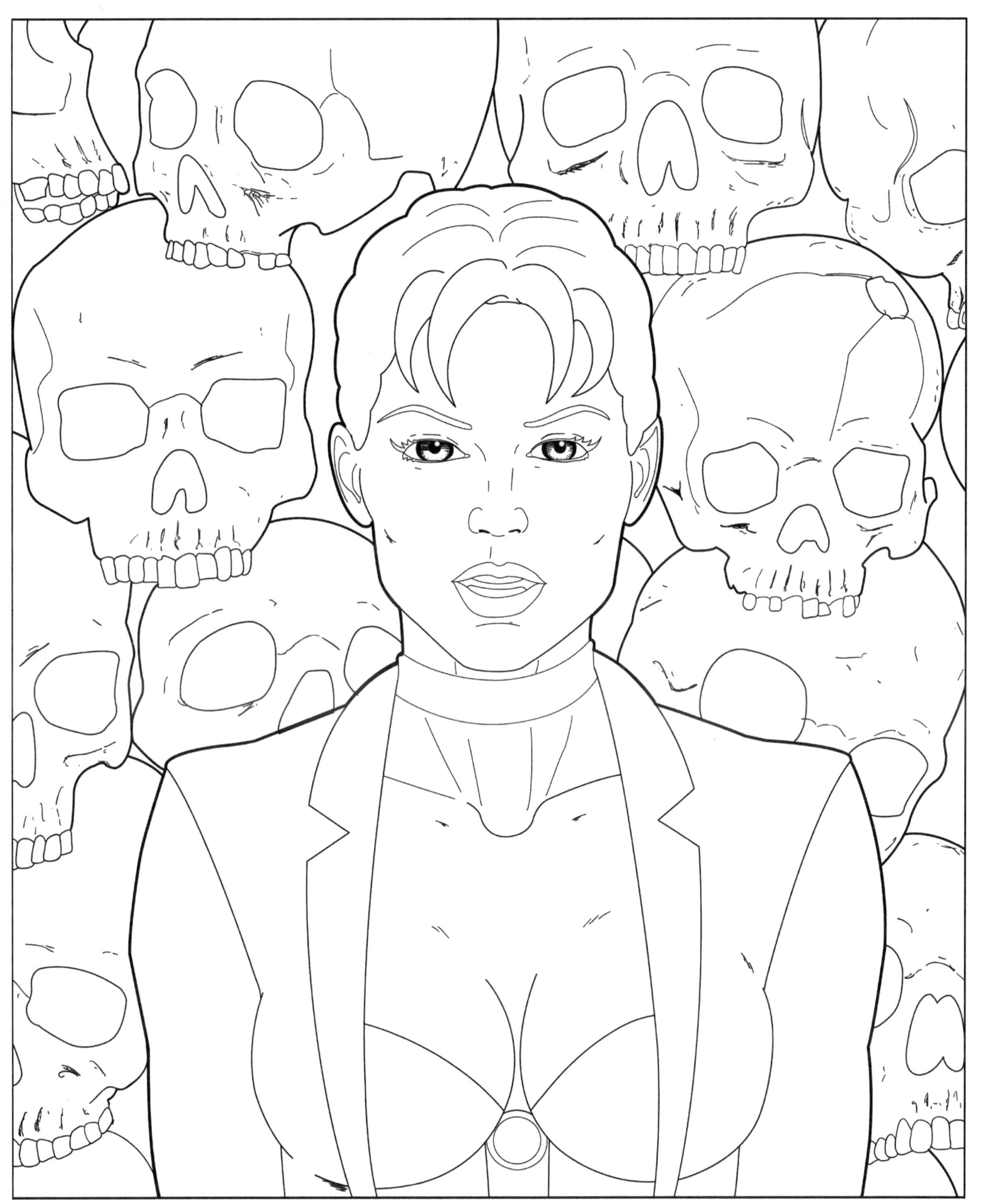

After a massacre, Friendly Corp collects the skulls for a final body count.

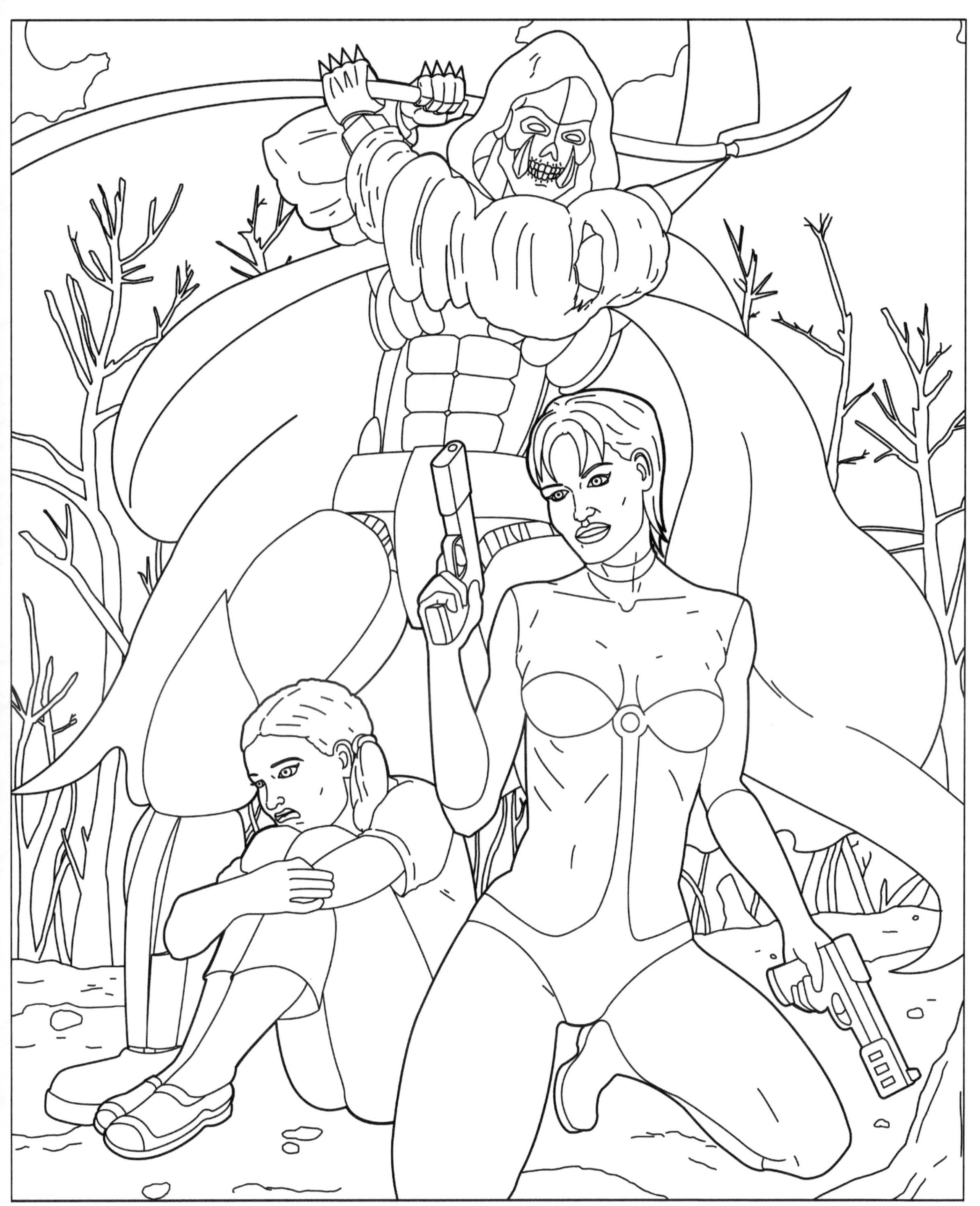

An early cover art concept for Mars Gambit issue 2.

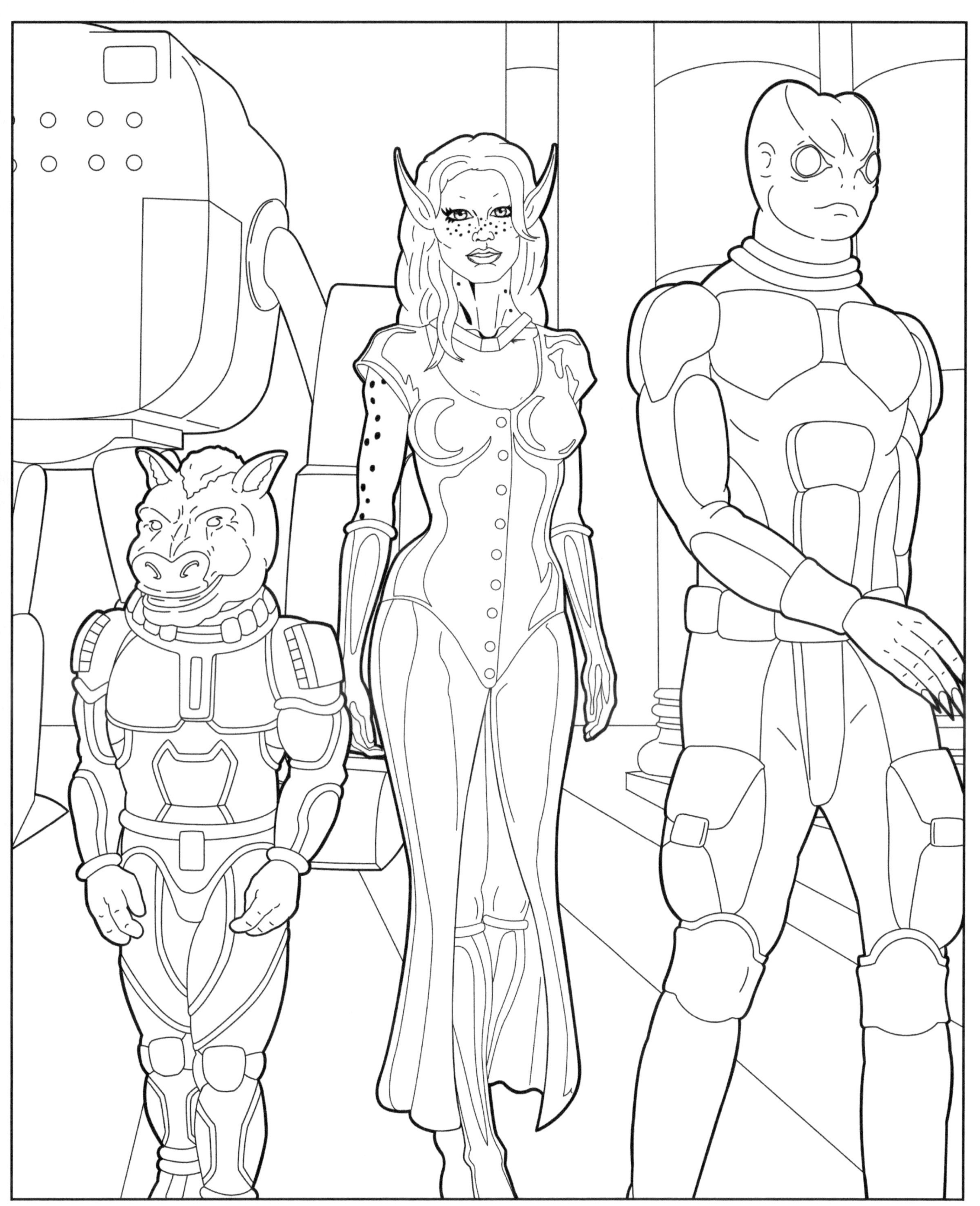

Cabbie, Soo Mi, and a local on a street in Cray City.

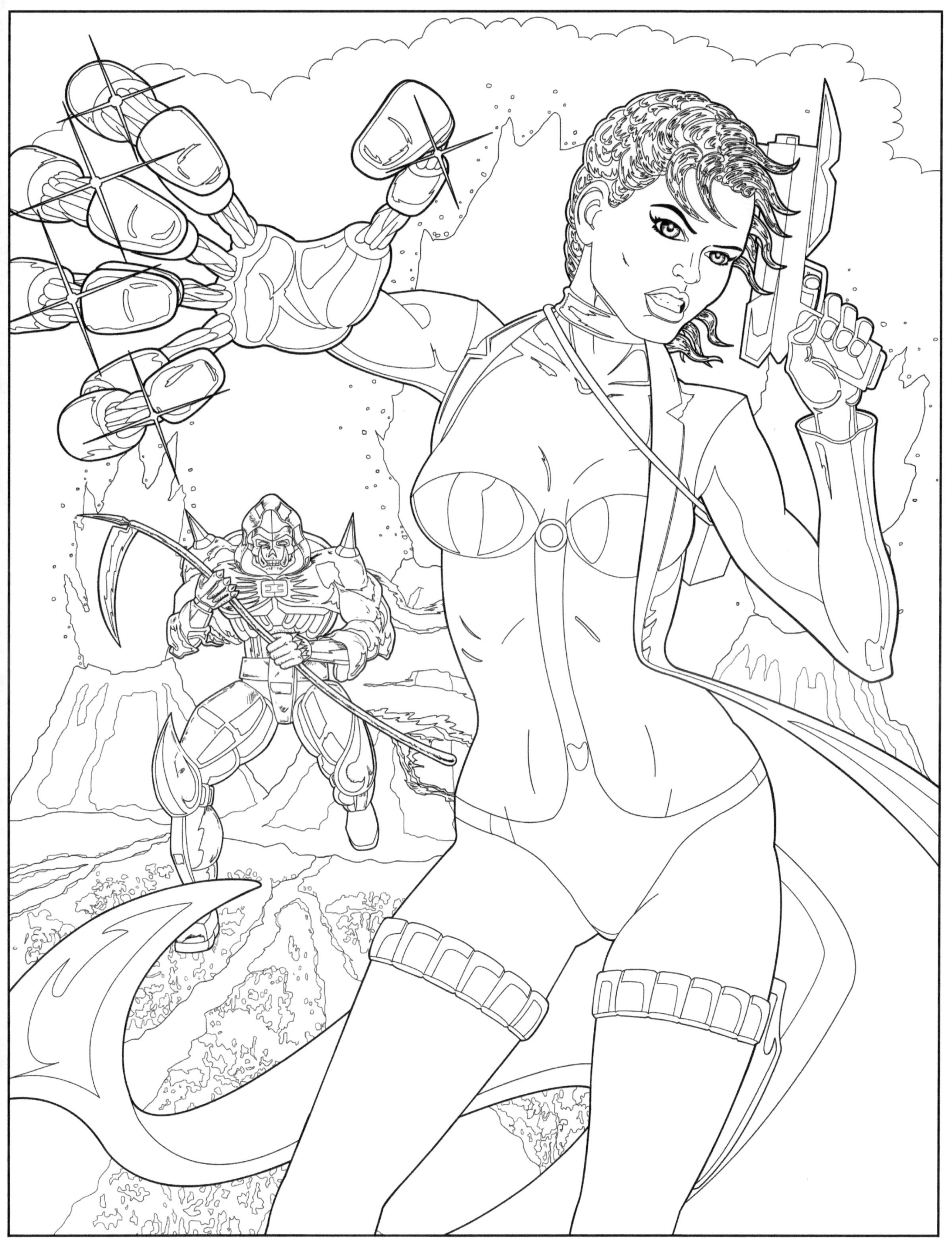

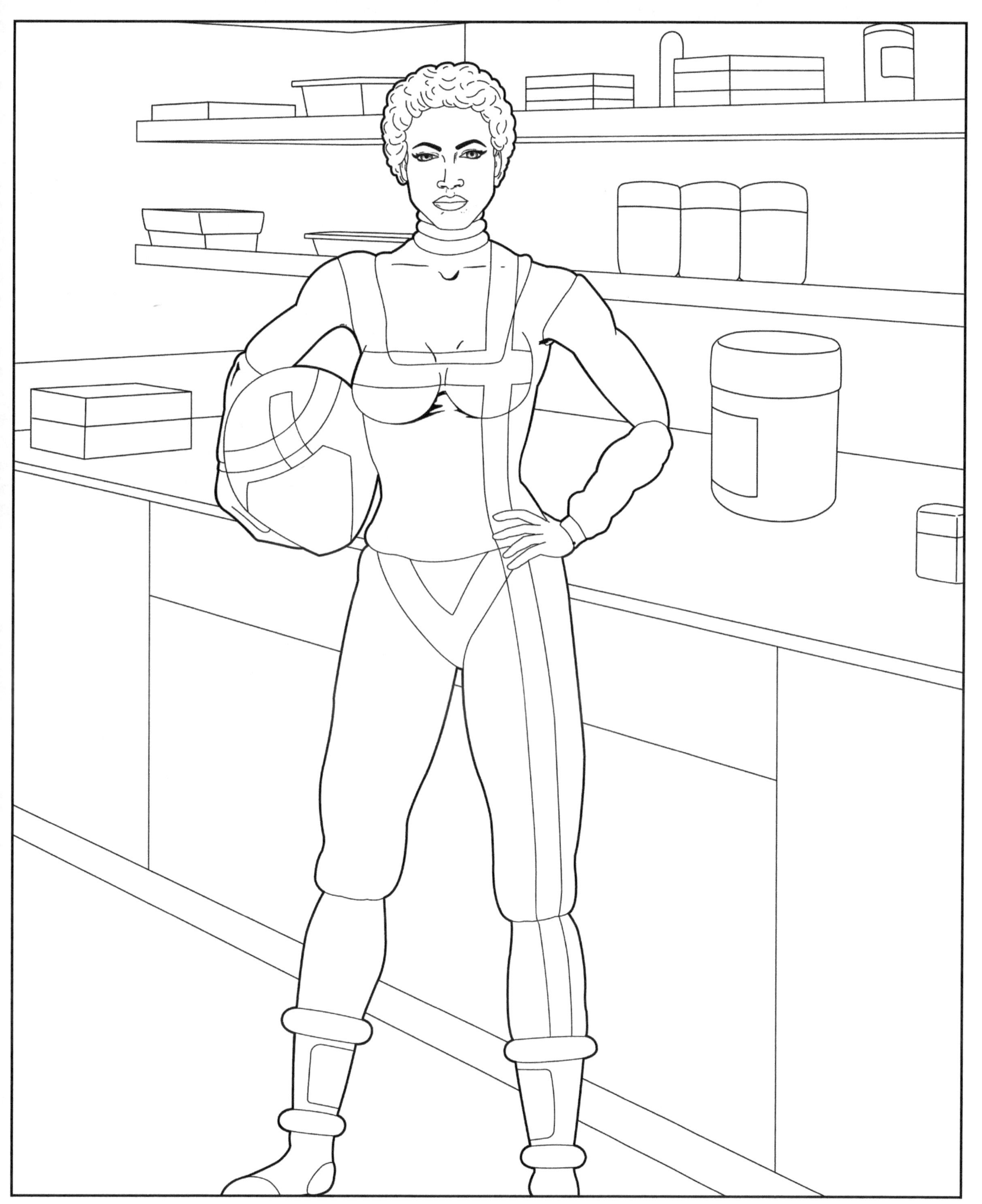

Ximena Jackson is the lead scientist developing new Salesman Assassins.

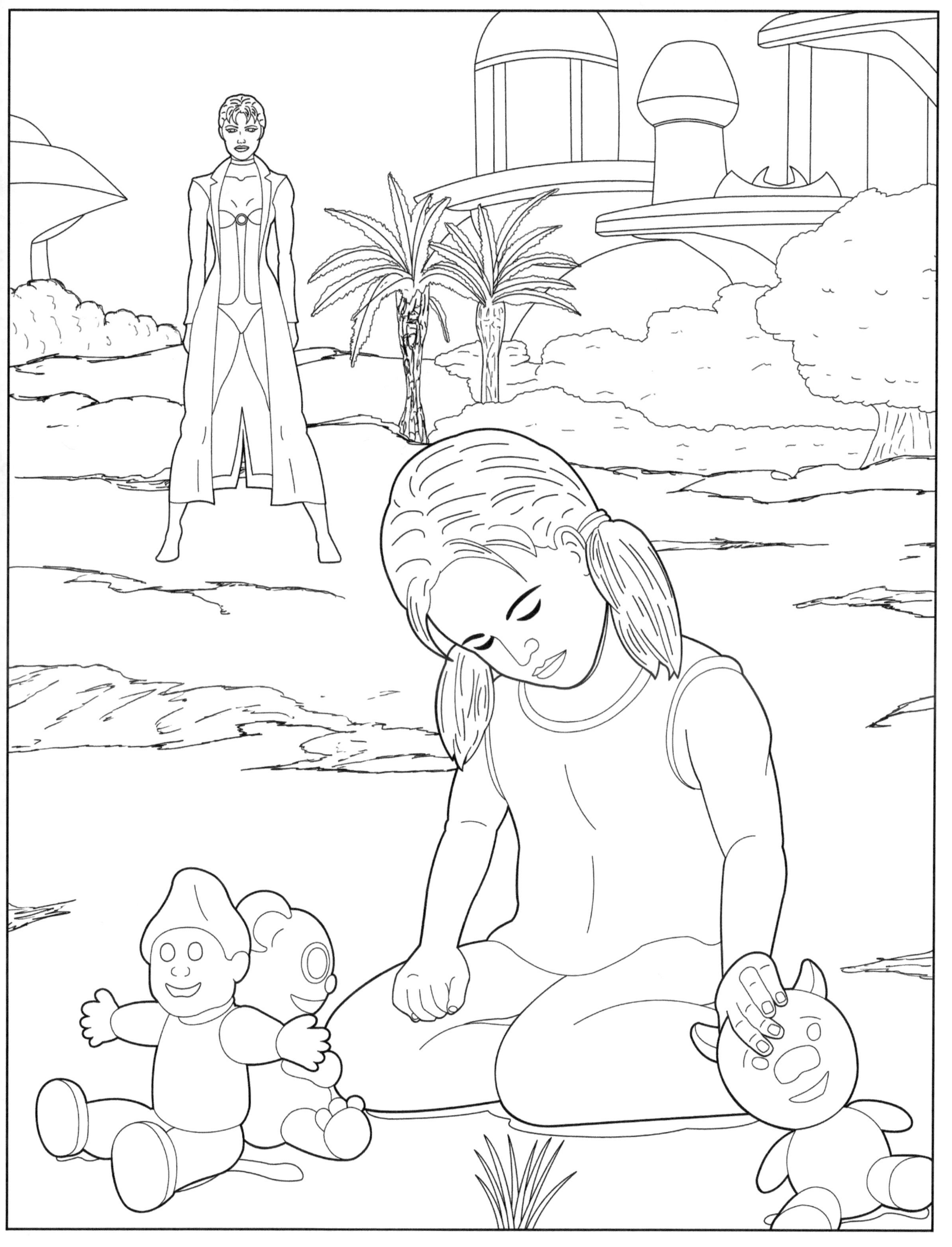

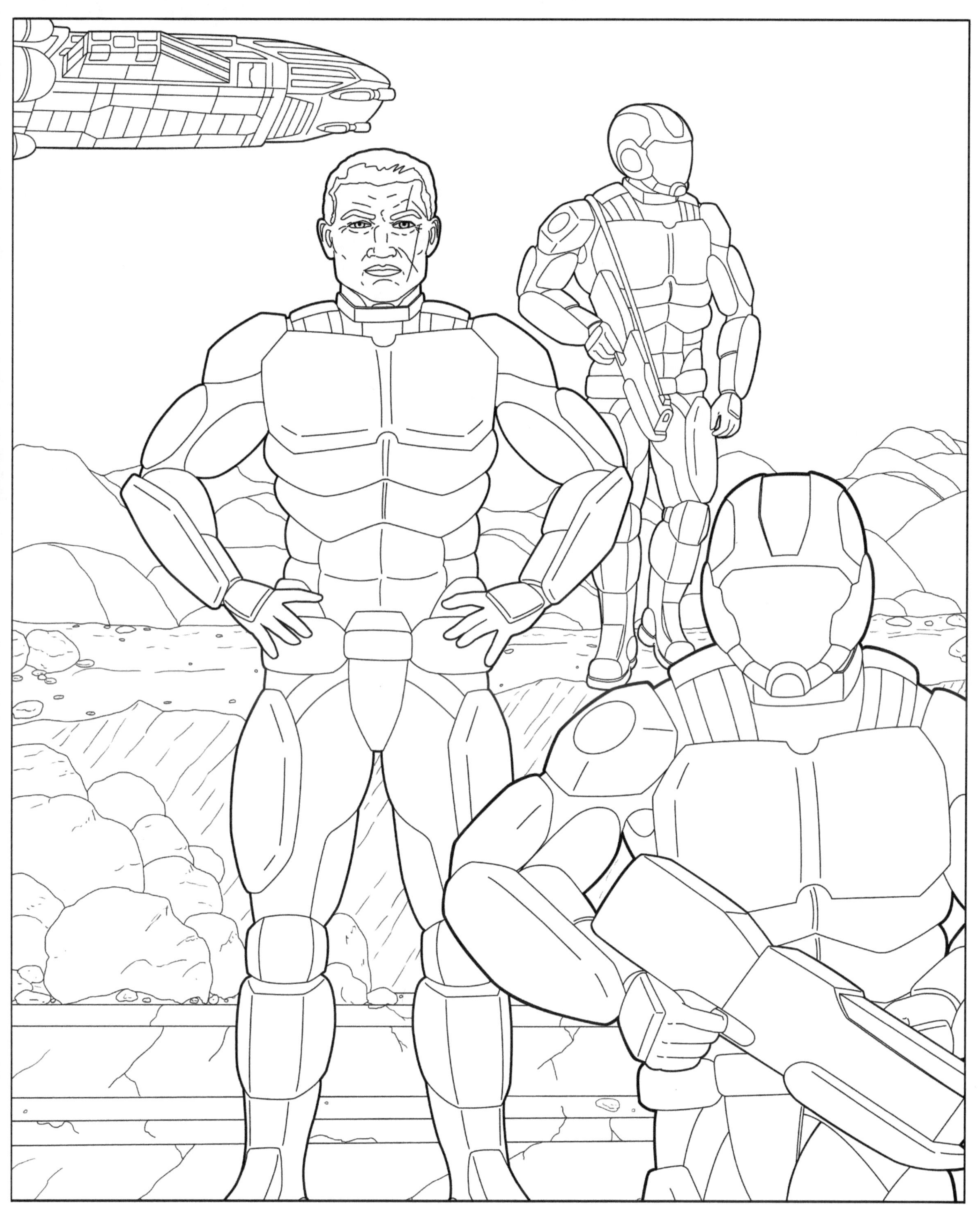

General Troy has fought both against and with Friendly Corp.

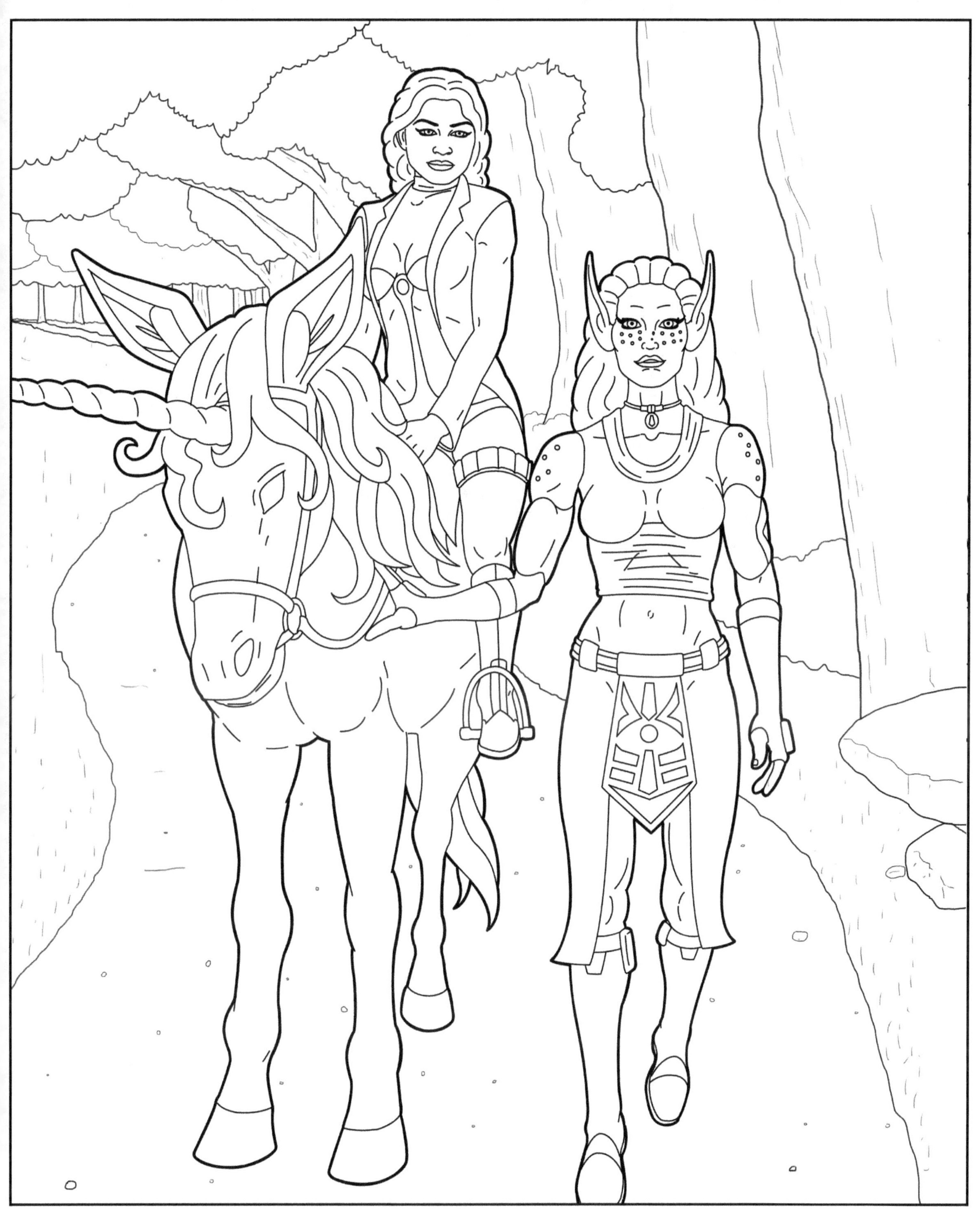

Sage and Kedves enjoy a walk on Perian Prime.

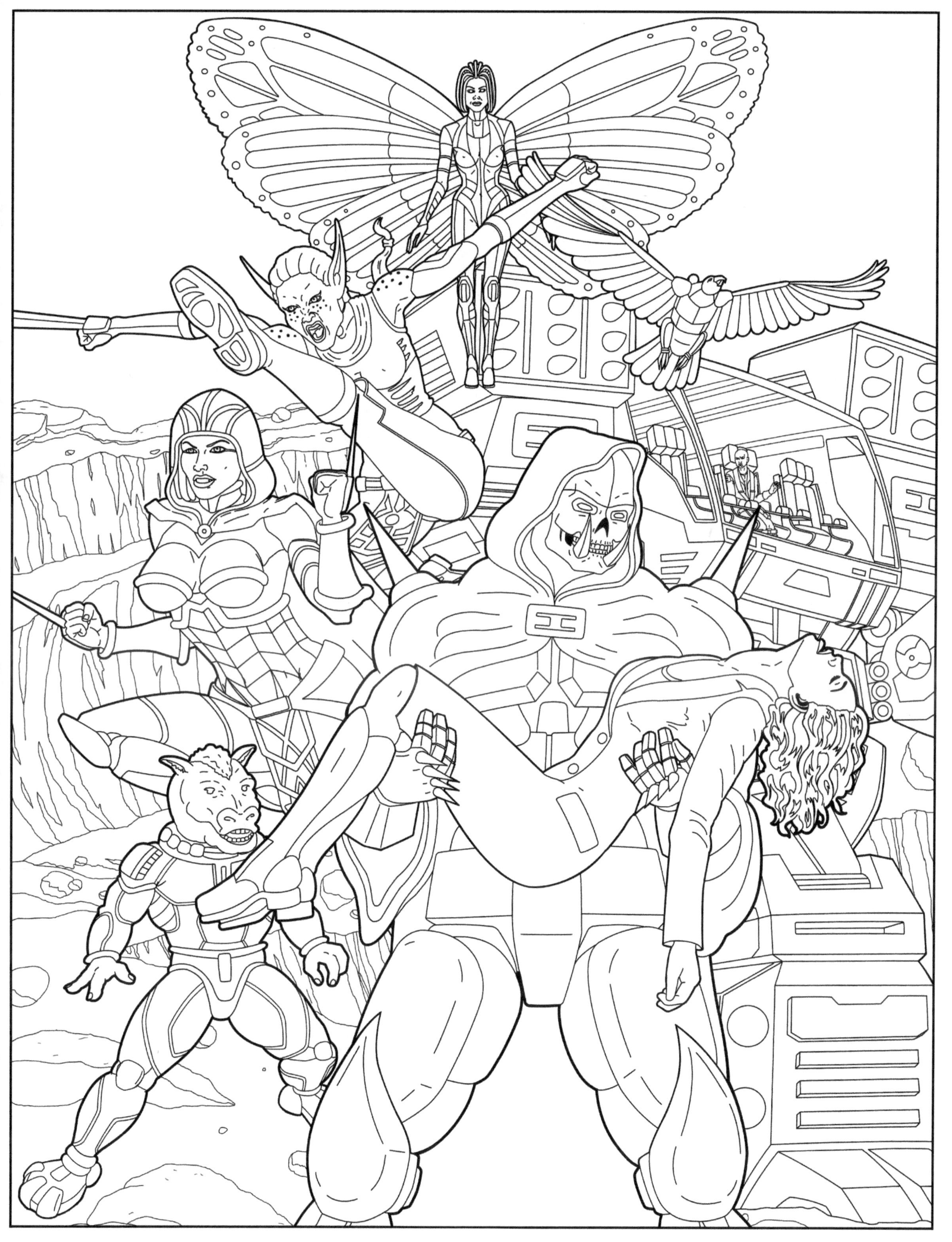

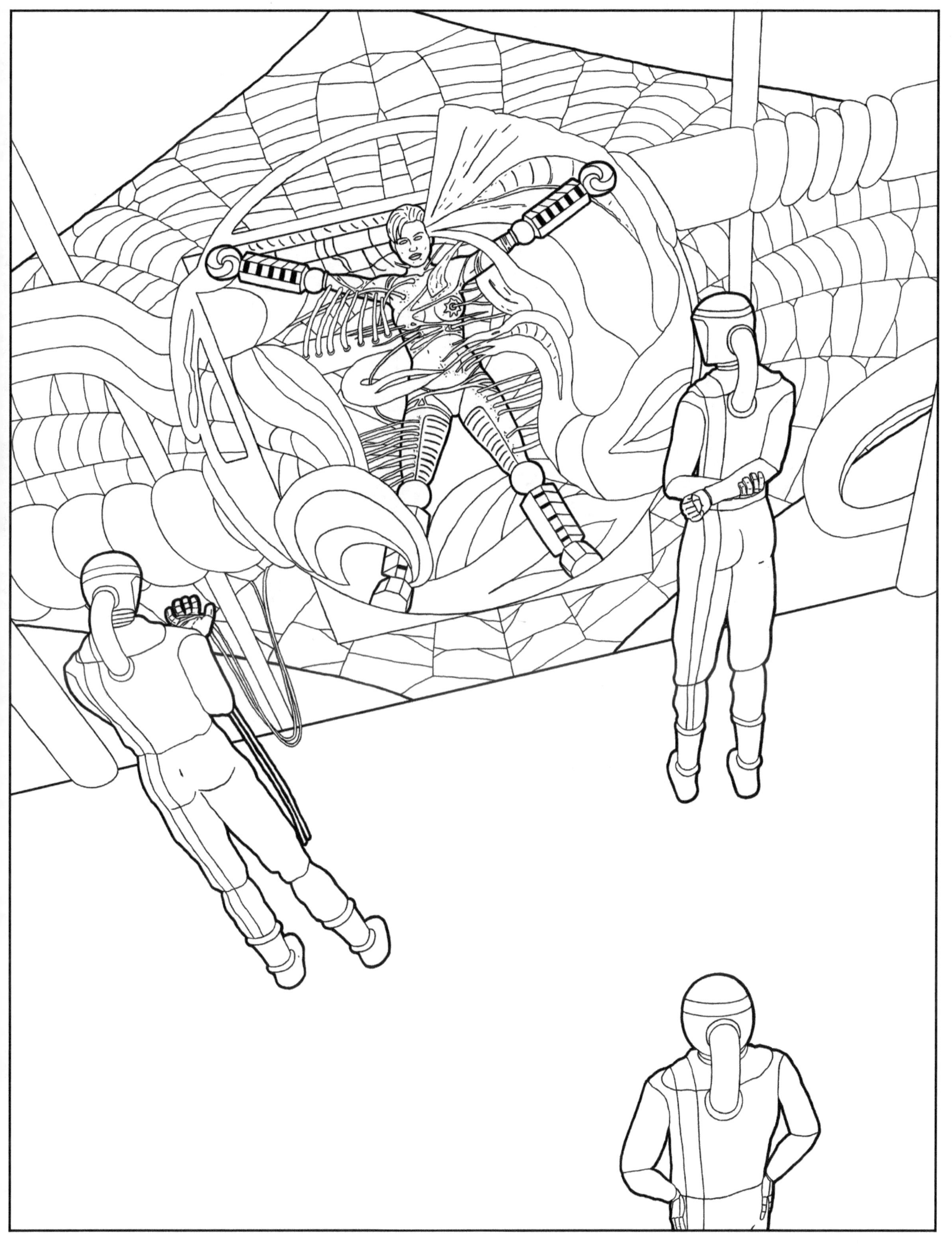

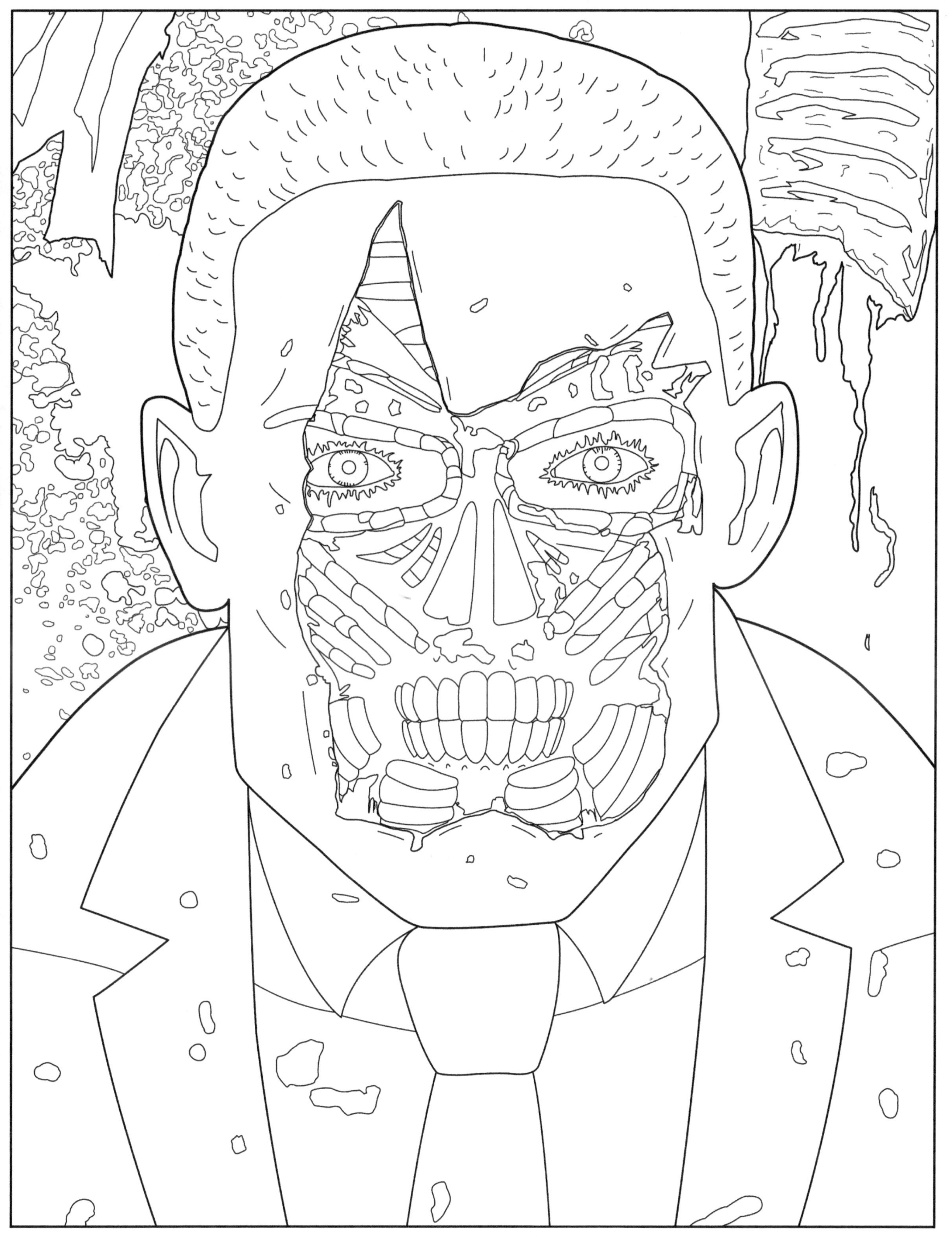

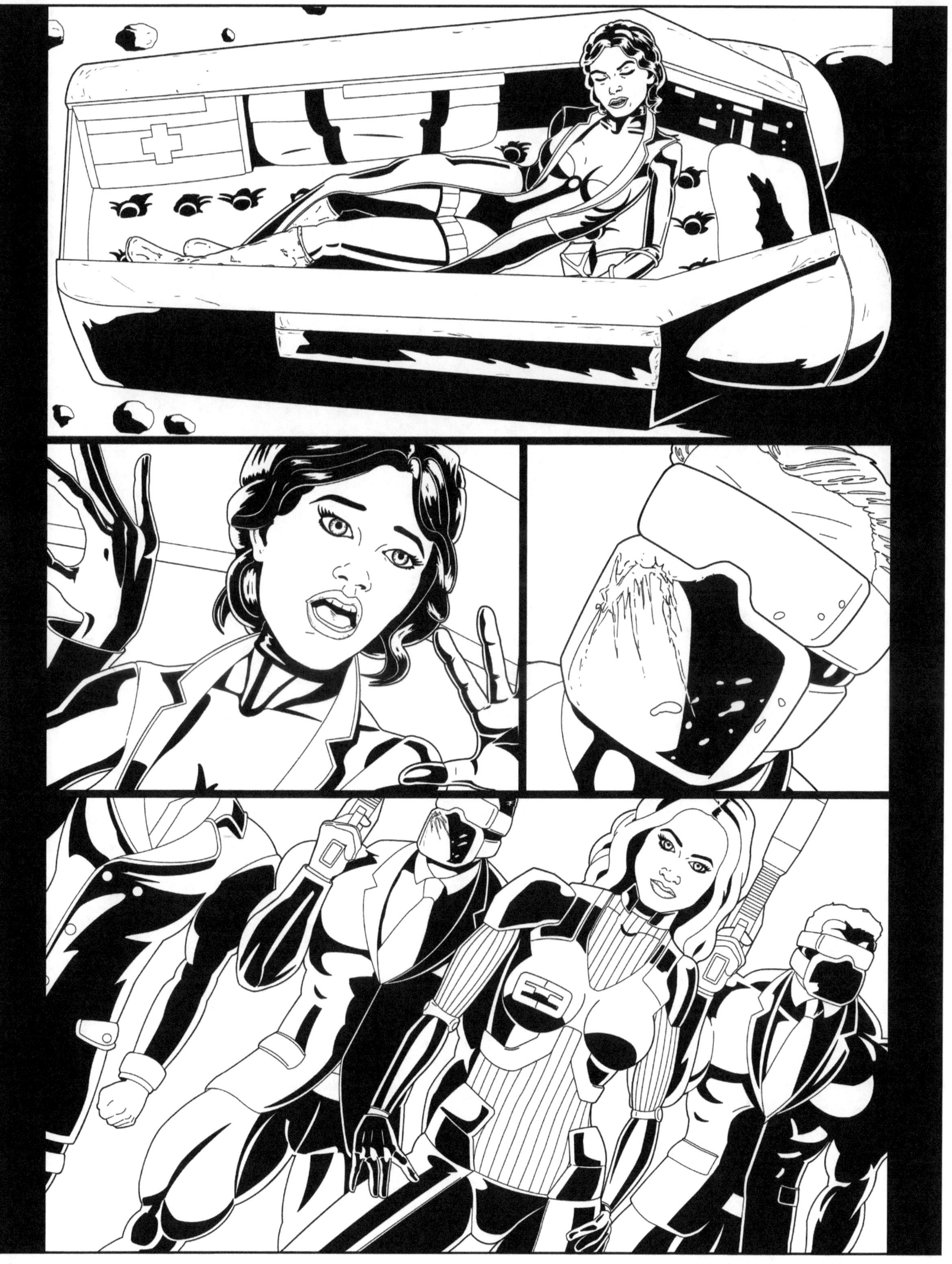

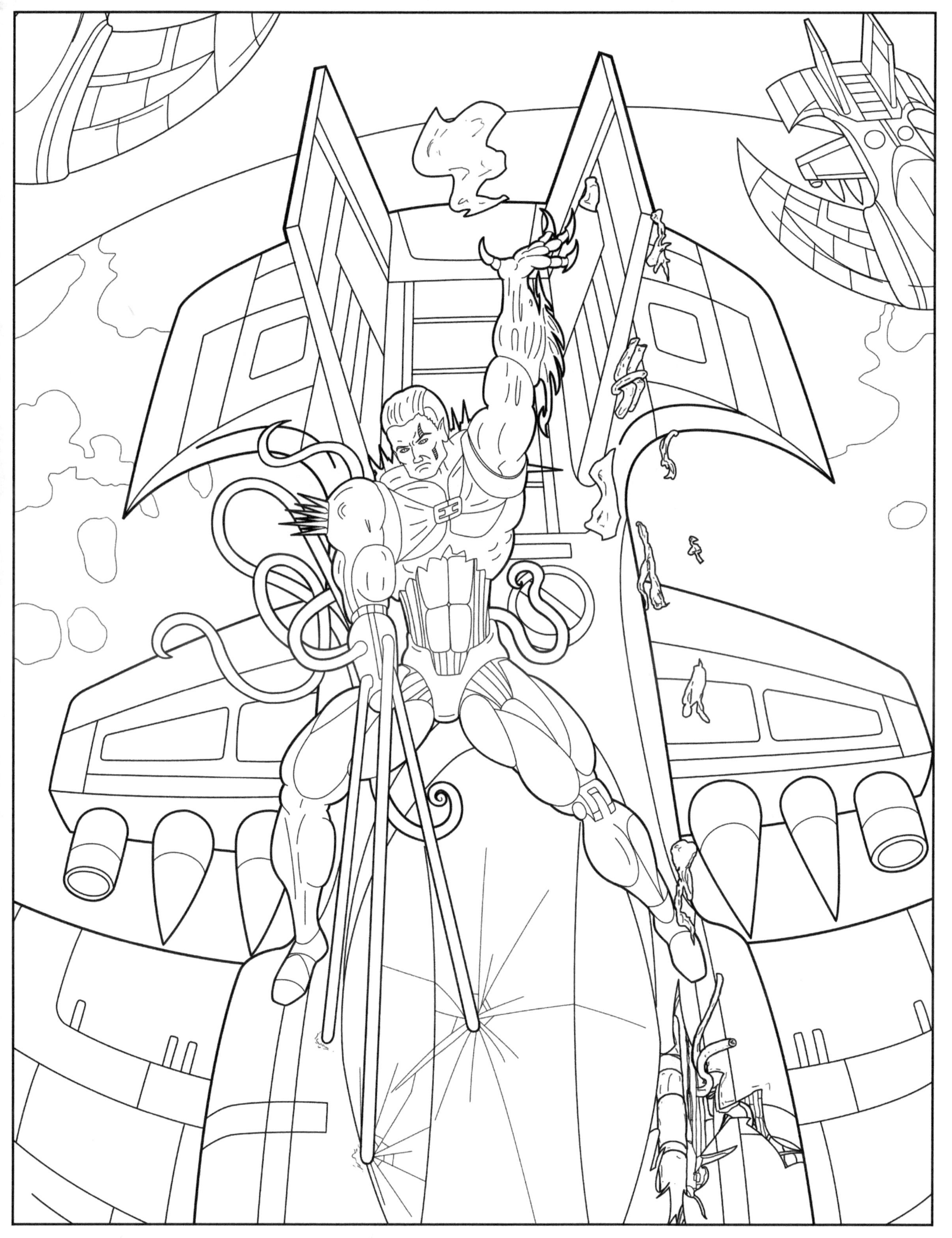

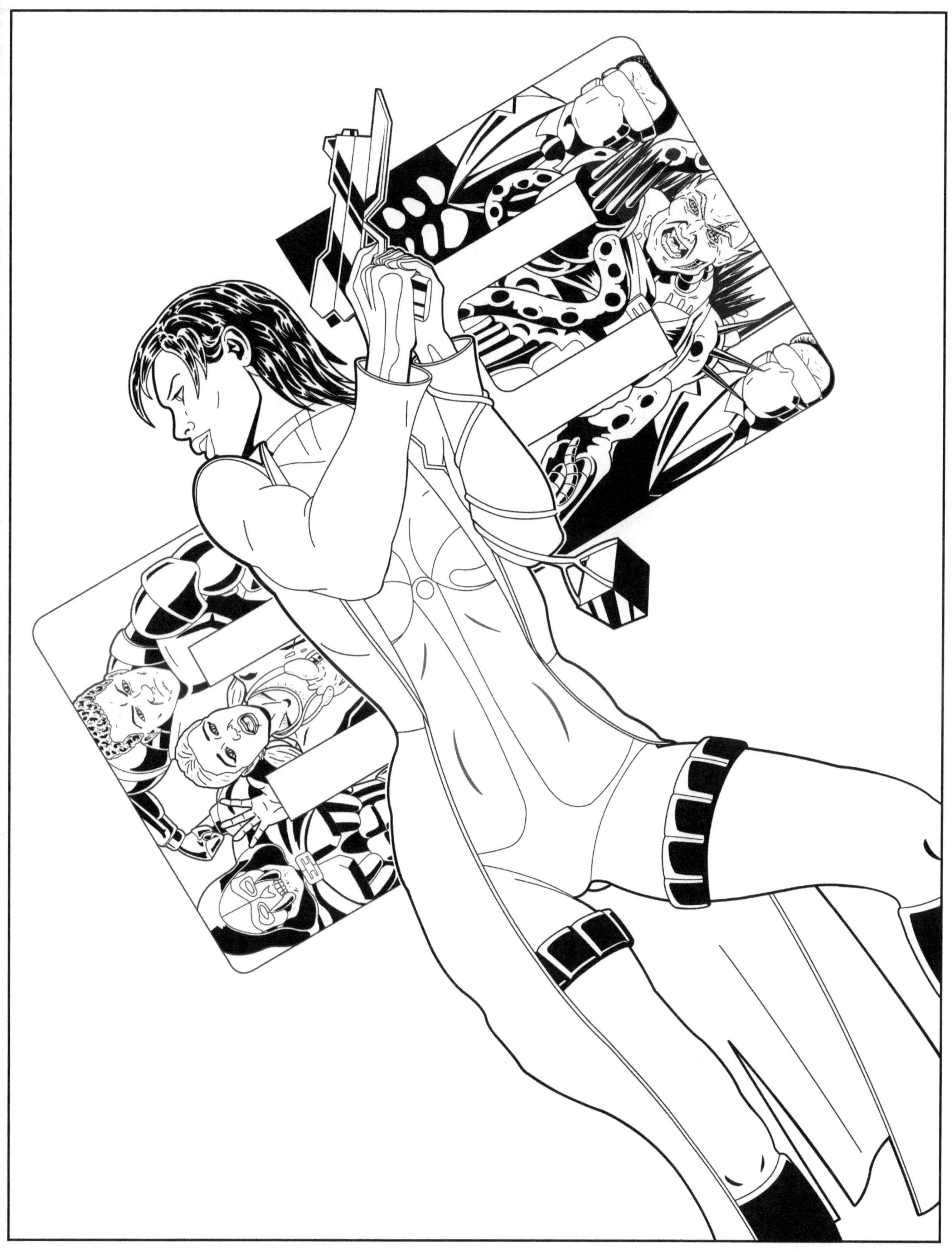

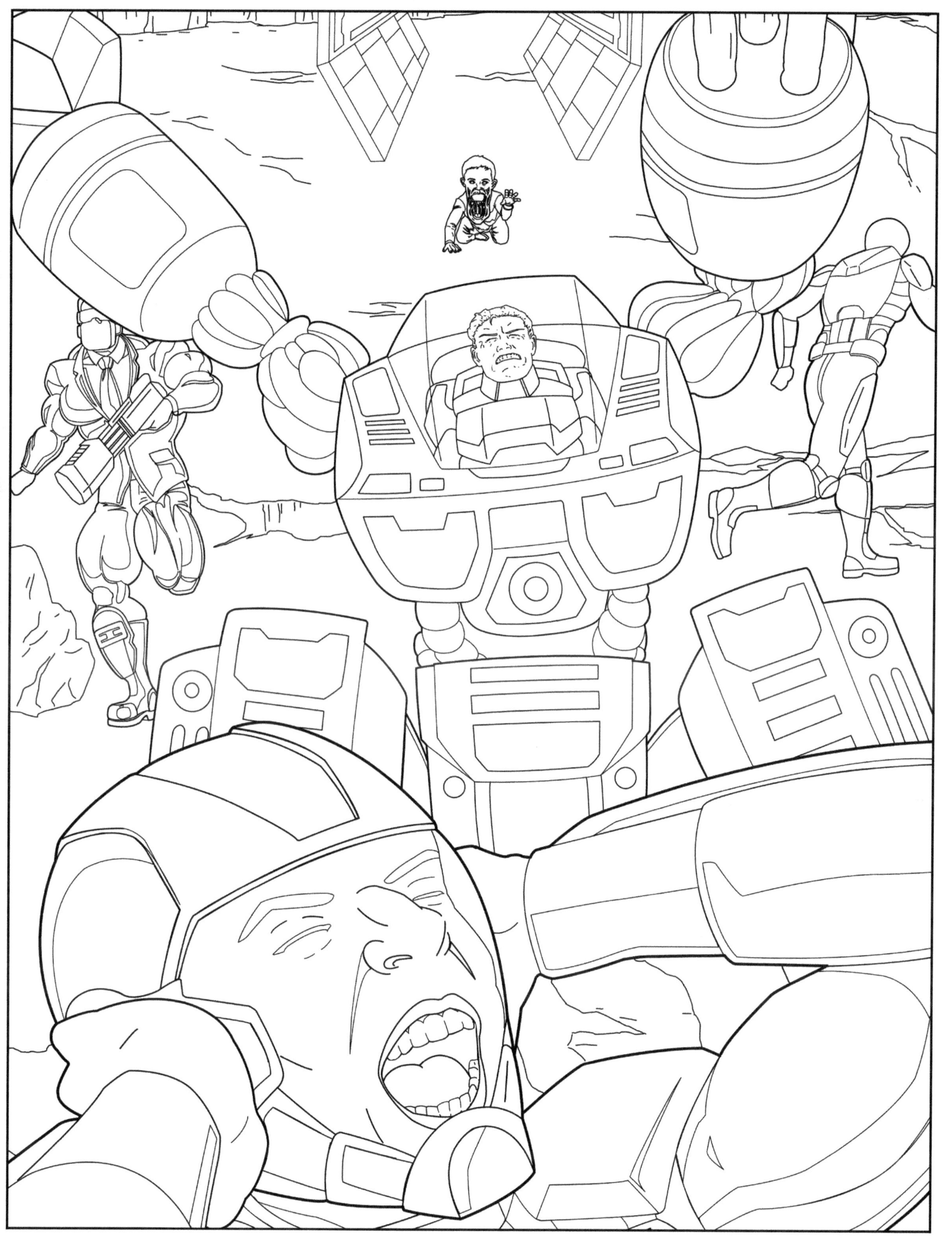

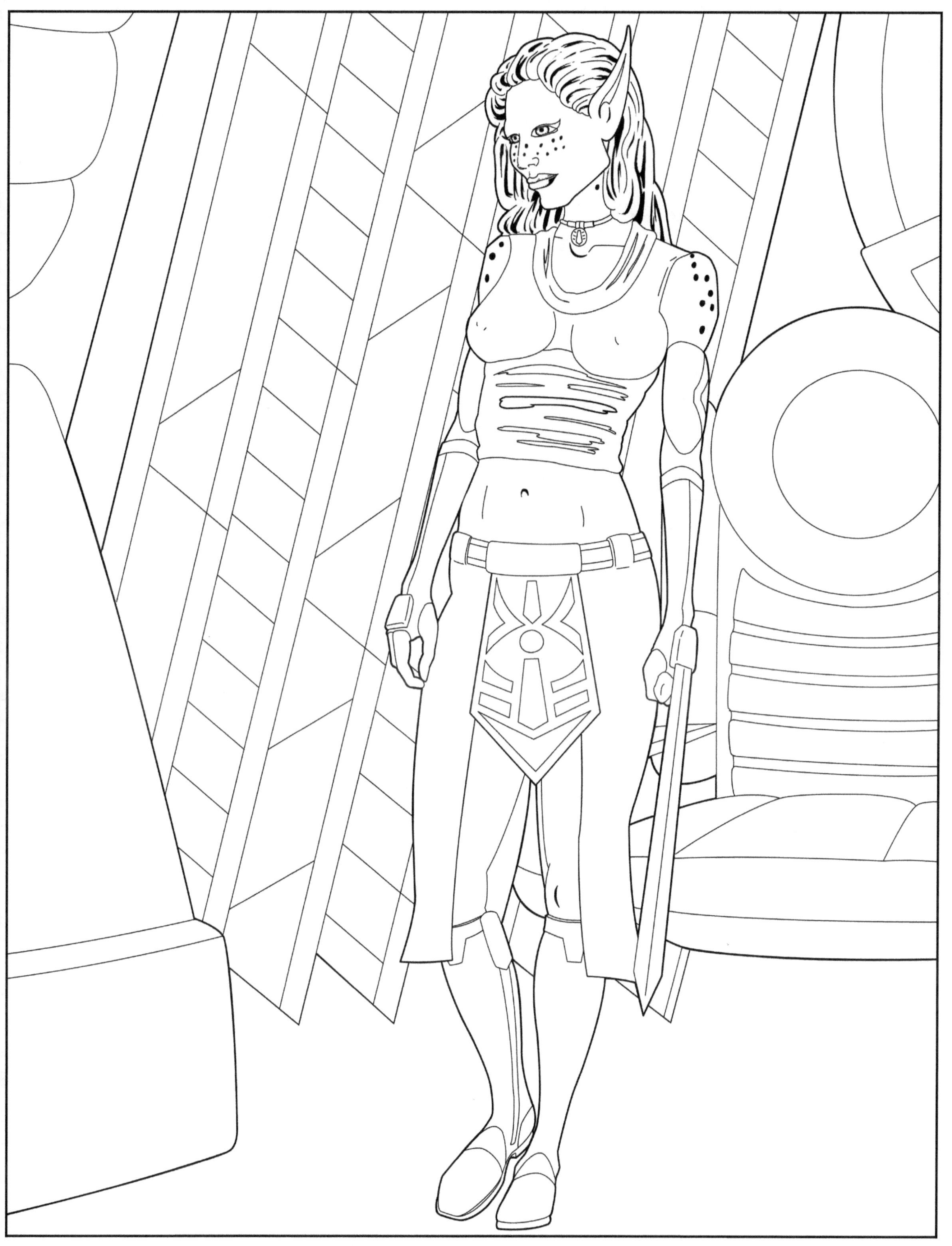

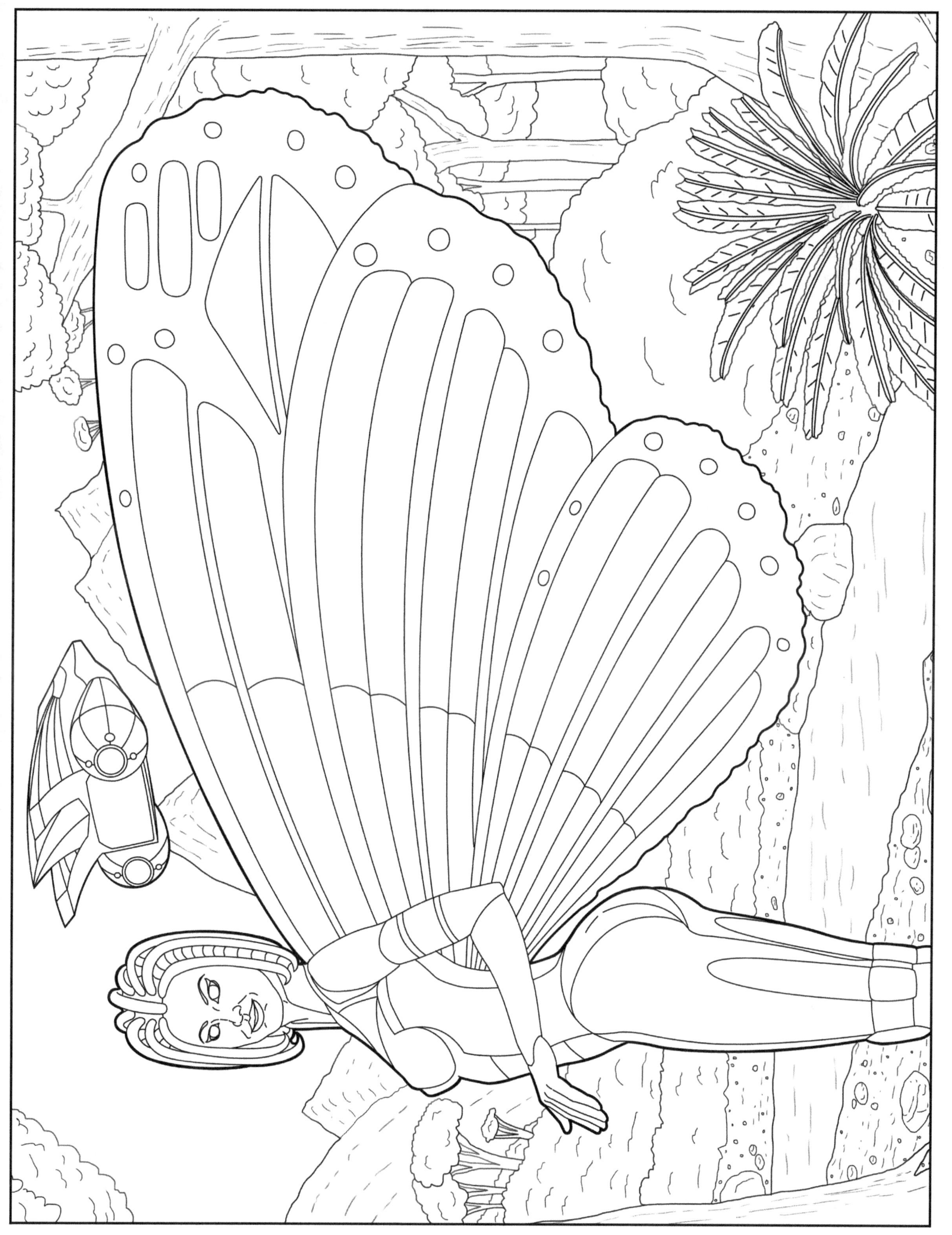

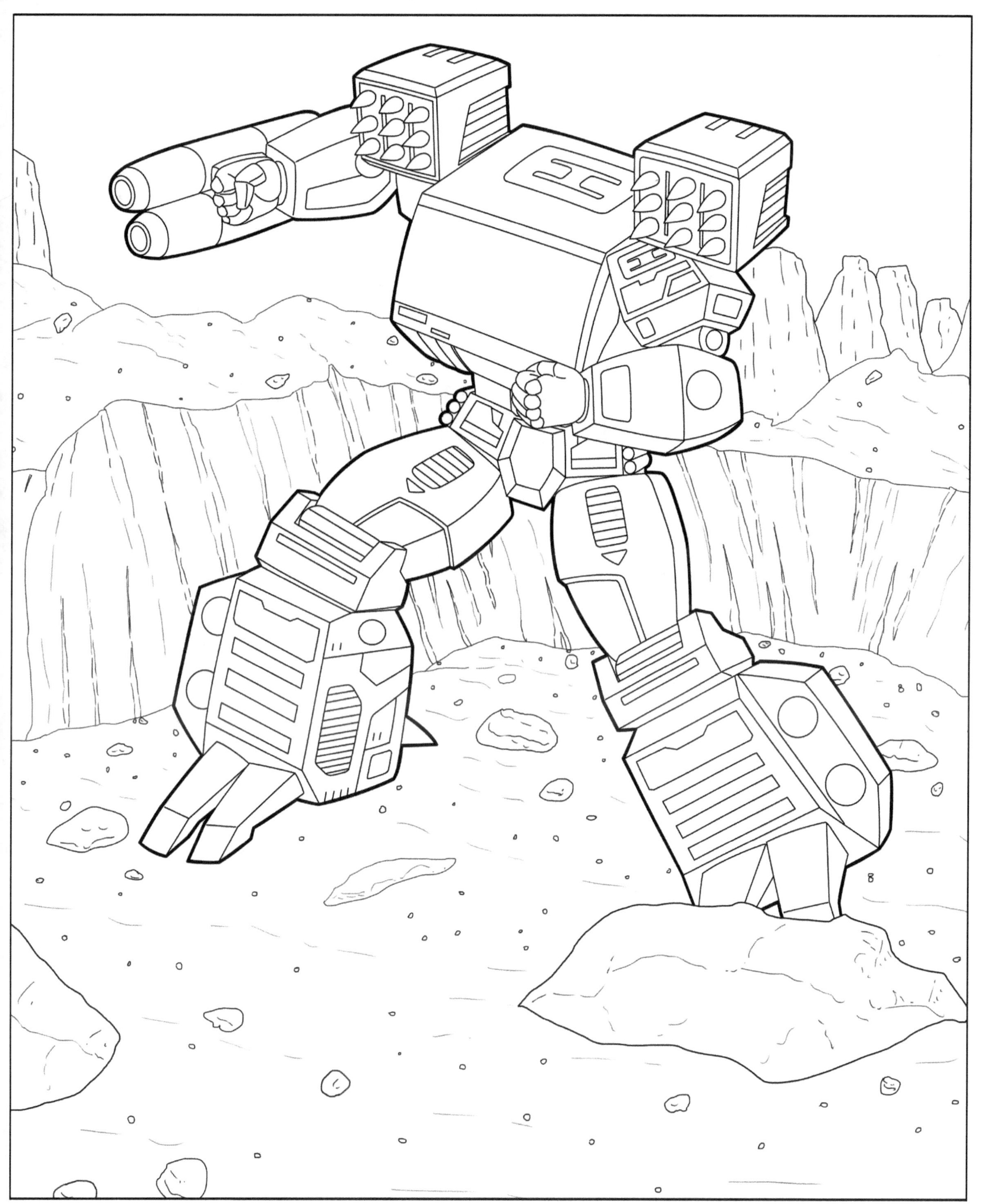

This Salesman Assassin shuttle has a mech-suit robot mode for combat.

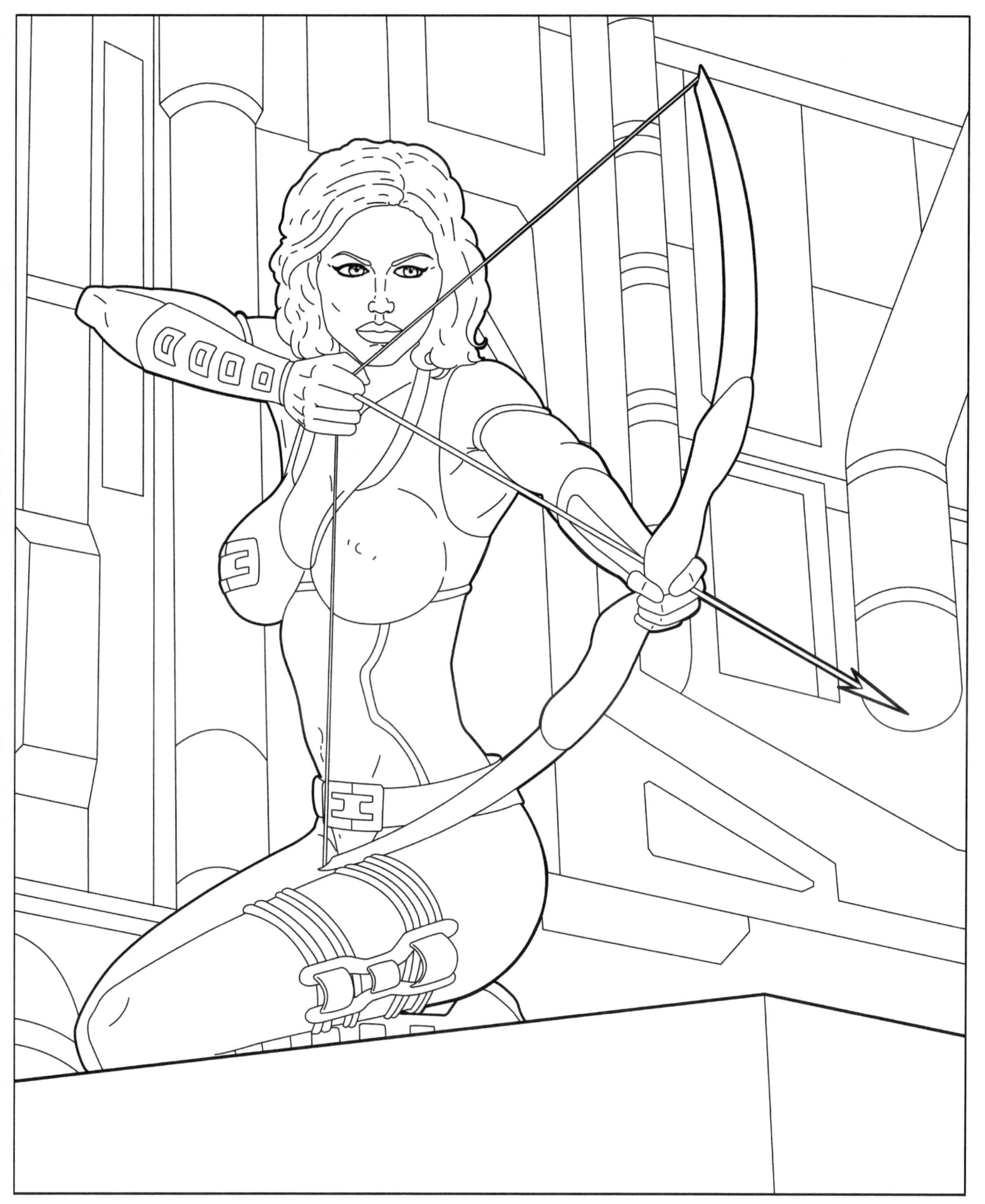

Honey is part of the new wave of Salesman Assassins.

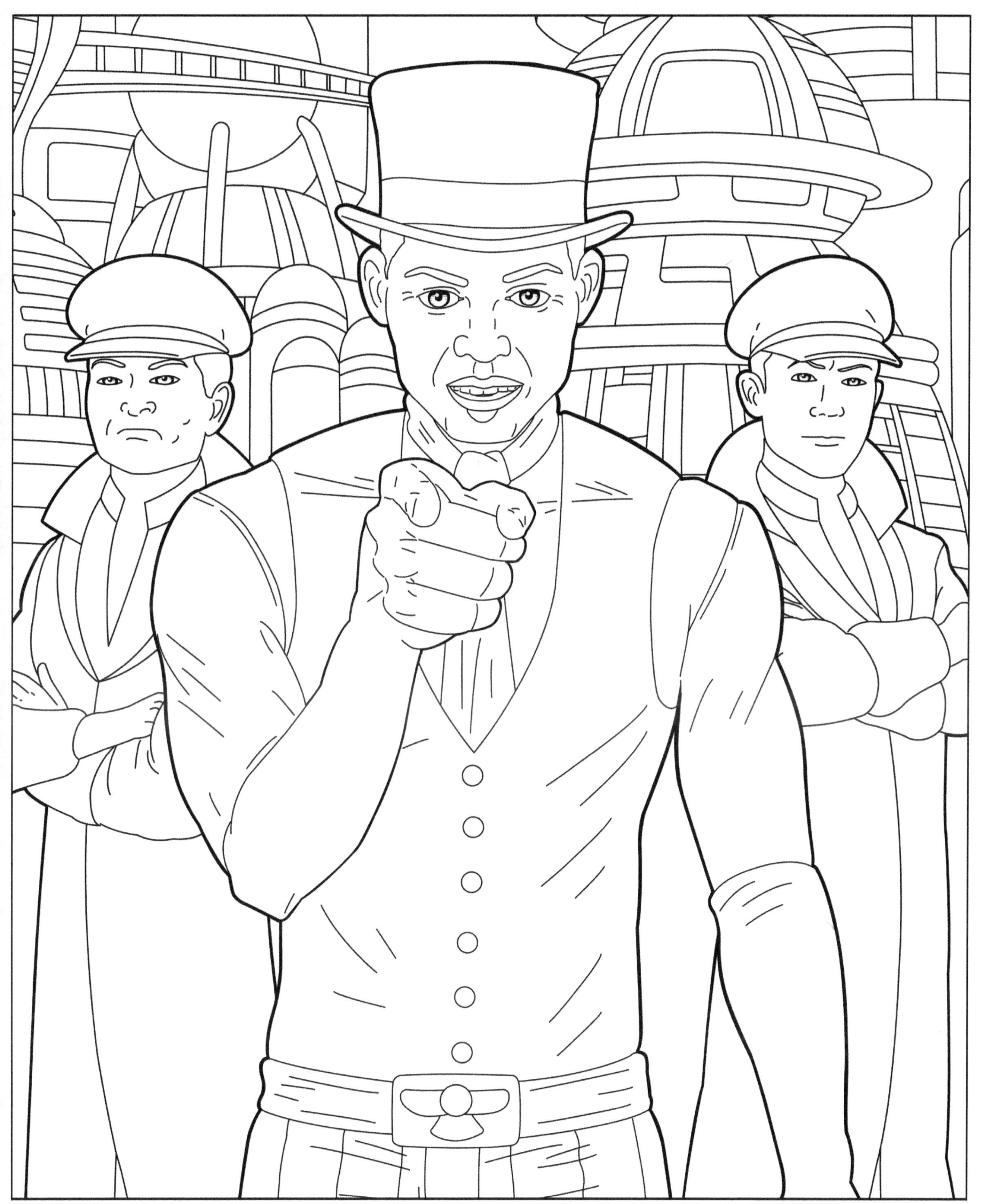

Elvis Cray has his own city that floats above Mars.

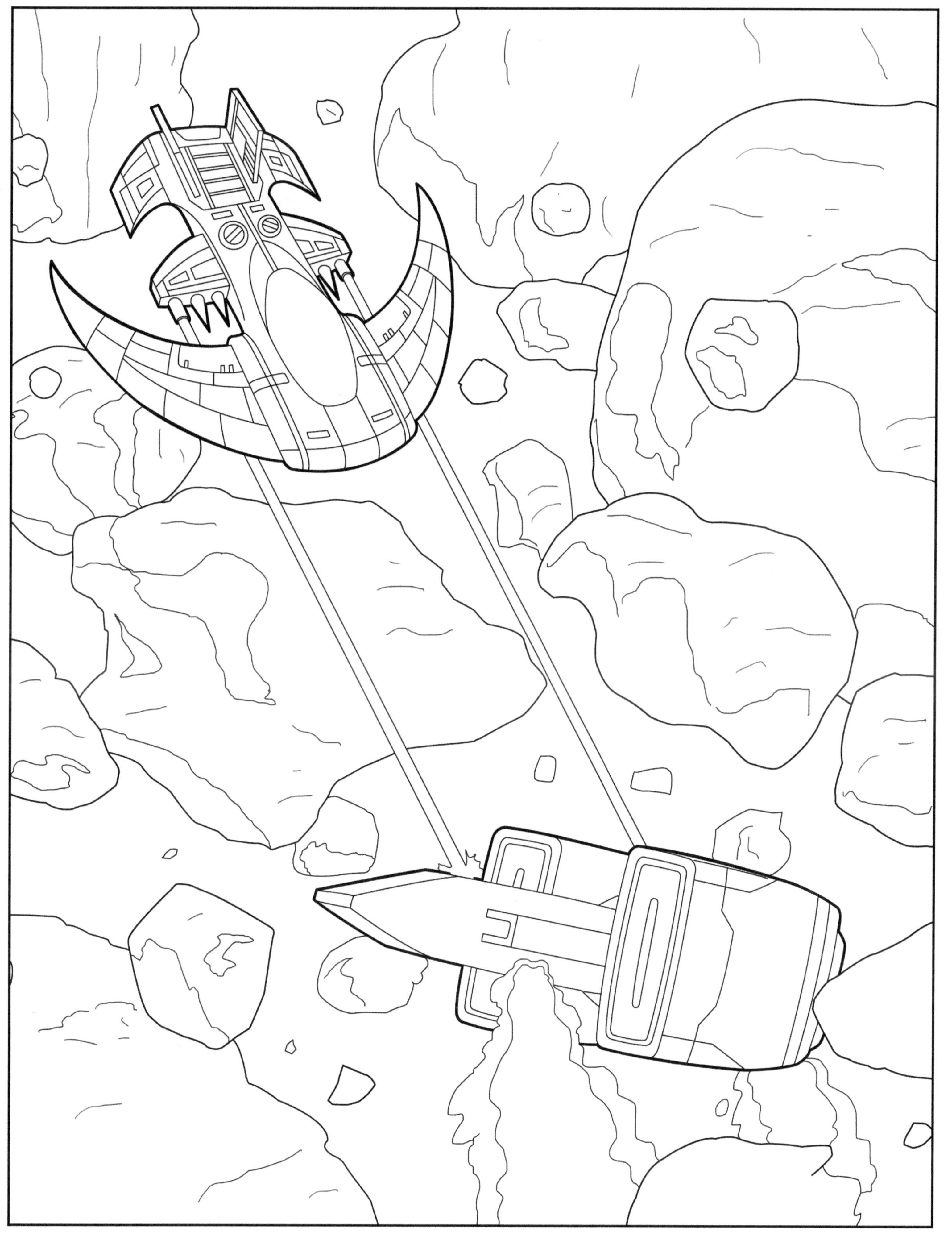

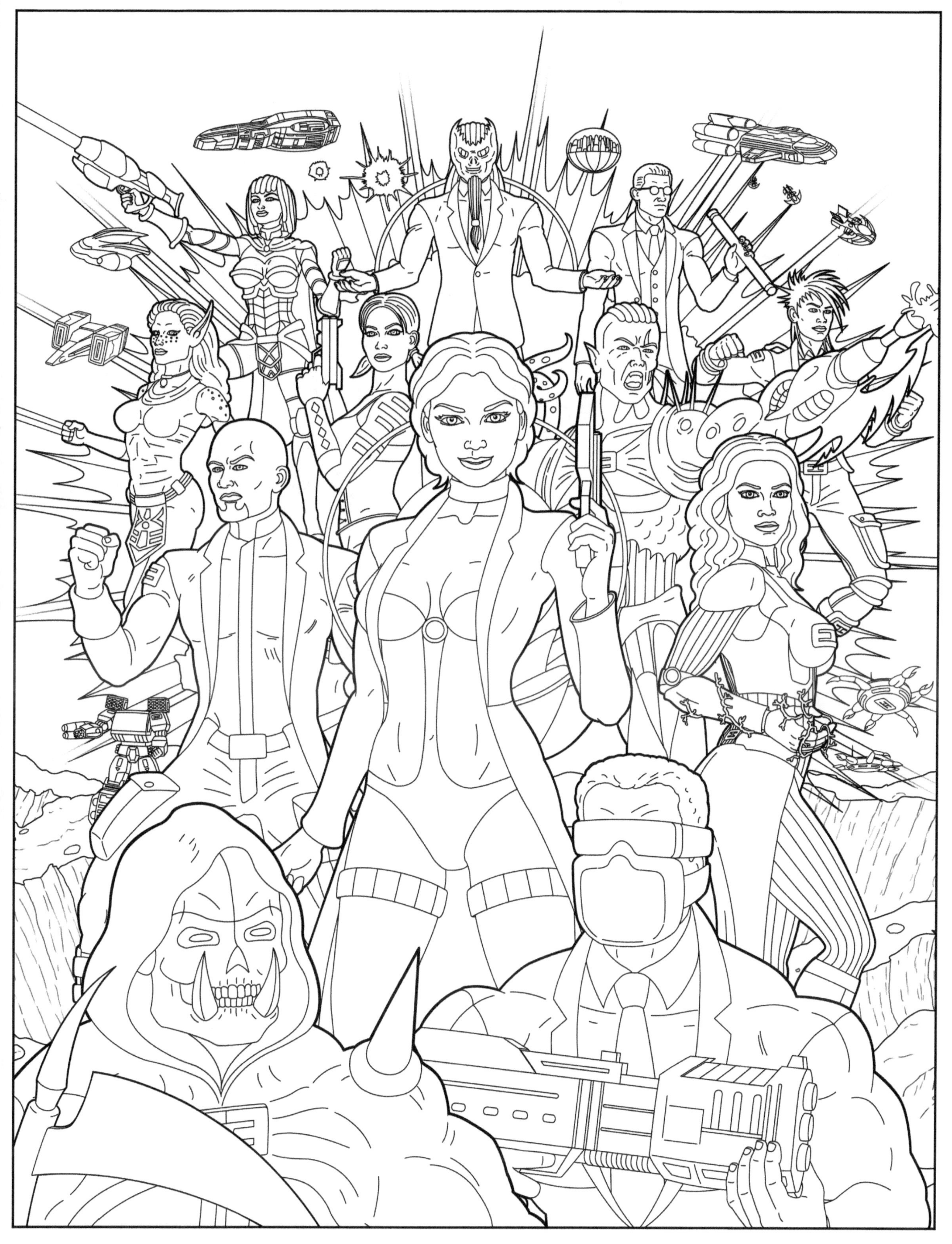

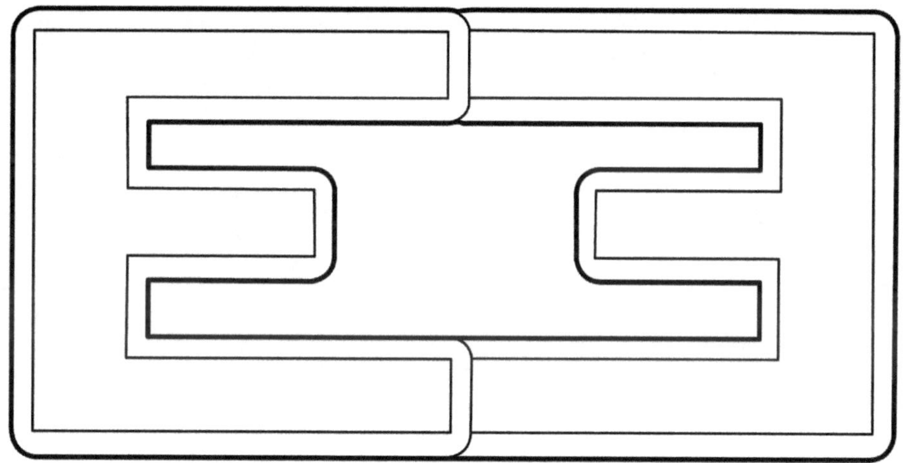

www.ingramcontent.com/pod-product-compliance
Lightning Source LLC
LaVergne TN
LVHW081416110826
845149LV00010B/1758
9780994254924